Rocks, Paper, Flowers

Rocks, Paper, Flowers

Carol, wishing you a happy & healthy New Year! Katie Sullivan

a novel by

Katie Sullivan

Holladay House Publishing

Holladay House Publishing

Holladay House Publishing
1120 Bancroff Lane
Manning, SC 29102

First edition, first printing 2014

Book and jacket design by Abby Sink
Author photo by Scott Henderson
Manufactured in the United States of America

Hardback edition ISBN 978-0-9900091-8-4

Trade Paperback edition ISBN 978-0-9900091-9-1

Acknowledgments

Darla Walls, you're a true friend! Thank you for your support and encouragement when I needed it most. (Especially at the book signing on Daufuskie Island…God bless Donna.) "I'm really not this social."

Thank you, Amy Daniell, for being the best friend a person could have. Stacey Quarrick, thank you for putting up with me every day at work. You're a saint, and I promise no more tears.

Beth McDowell, Stacy Newton, Jennie, Ginny, Linda, Kate, Susie, Jessie, Tina, Dana, Ricky, Beth S., Beth N., and Ms. Morton: Y'all got me through a very difficult year, and I will always be thankful.

A huge thank you goes to my Uncle John who read every rough draft of mine, especially when he didn't have time. I will always be grateful. You hold a special place in my heart.

Maureen, Molly, and Suson—thank you for giving me the funny material to write. I can't wait until our next trip…I heard Pete's paying for it.

Last but not least, I want to thank my incredible editor and publisher Holly Holladay. You are amazingly talented, and you inspire me to be a better writer. Thank you for believing in me and making a lifetime dream come true.

437… Jump in, the water feels great!

Dedication

For my children—Bailey, Erin, and Sullivan. You three are every-thing that I value in my life. I love you punks, and I'm incredibly lucky to be your mom. Give me two, right here.

Table of Contents

Chapter One

June 4, 2011

My body felt numb, but my heart still felt the pain. I sat at the kitchen table and poured another glass of cabernet. I picked up the picture of Mom and me when I was ten years old with her arms wrapped around me. Her big, contagious smile was infectious. She looked so happy. Life was good then, and I didn't even know it. Now though, my heart was breaking piece by piece, and I was more determined than ever to drink away the pain and emptiness I had suffered for so many years. My mind played a slide show of the past with visions of my mother's body in her coffin, and I couldn't find the pause button. My goal again tonight was to get plastered and to forget my pain, to forget my past, and to forget about my overwhelming grief. I picked up my wine glass and stumbled out the back door to the patio to look for my cigarettes and lighter. I always put them in a new hiding place, so no one would know my dirty secret. I lifted the seat cushion on the wicker sofa, grabbed both of them, and positioned my chair so no one in the house could see what I was doing.

The kids had been sleeping for hours, and Tom was upstairs watching TV. Still, I didn't want to be discovered. This was my time, my sadness, and my chance to wallow about my past. No one understood.

I smoked the cigarette in the black of night as I pulled the rosary out of my pocket and rubbed a single bead back and forth with my thumb and first finger. I didn't pray the rosary very often, but it was the back and forth movement, almost like a mother rocking her baby, that gave me peace. It was the only thing that gave me comfort when I reached this level of sorrow. The rosary made of red roses was the closest thing I had to my mother besides the pictures that haunted me. I exhaled the smoke from my mouth and watched it rise as I looked up to the stars beaming in the night sky. "I'm sorry I let you down, Mom," I said as I started to cry.

My mother died on Christmas Day back in 1985. I was sixteen years old: old enough to know what was happening but also too young to understand the impact that it would have on me for the rest of my life. I had been grieving for so long that it felt normal. *Was I ready to let it go?* It didn't matter if I was or wasn't. I was going back to my mother's grave in two days with my sisters. This trip marked my first visit in fourteen years.

Every year, we take a sisters' trip. My younger sister, Fiona, is a world traveler, and she always chooses our destination. However, this year is a little different. Fiona and my older sister Helen decided that we should return to my mother's grave. I know they are doing this for me. When my mother died, Helen was in college. Fiona was only eleven years old. I don't know if it was that Helen was older and stronger and Fiona was younger and didn't understand as well, but they handled my mother's death with a strength and grace I don't possess. I have been plagued with an unshakable guilt for the past twenty-five years. So this trip is for Mom, but it is also for me. Helen and Fiona believe that it will help me heal.

We are traveling to Dubuque, Iowa, where my mother is buried, and we will visit her relatives while we are there. The entire trip will last only three days. My insides are a mess. I desperately want to be with my sisters, but I have been having panic attacks for the past several weeks whenever I imagine seeing Mom's grave. I stagger back inside and hunt for my phone. The room is spinning, but I must focus to find it. As soon as I locate it, I search through the contacts for Fiona's number, but I can't see through the tears that fill my eyes. *I'm not going. I'm cancelling,* I say to myself as I try to work up enough confidence to call my little sister. *I can't go because I can't deal with this shit! I can't do this, and I'm just going to tell her.* I teeter to the sofa, thinking about my mom, trying to keep my eyes open. They feel so heavy, and I struggle. I don't want to go to her grave. *Nothing will change,* I think to myself. The wine officially takes over. The fight with my conscience ends, and I pass out on the sofa.

What seems like only a couple of minutes later, Tom wakes me up and tells me that coffee is ready. I watch as he picks up my cigarettes and lighter and walks them out to my hiding place. *How did he know?* I shake my head in disbelief, but it hurts too much, so I stop immediately. I can't hide anything: my feelings, my demons, my insecurities. I'm a mess. He walks back inside and reaches for my arm to help me up from the sofa. He calmly guides me toward the kitchen.

"You need to talk to somebody, Megan. You can't go on like this. It's too painful for me to watch. You get in these deep depressions about your mother, and it's like a black hole. I know that some days are better than others, but you have to get control of your emotions. It is getting worse. If you won't do it for yourself, do it for the kids. Did your mom ever act like this?"

"Shut up! Don't you dare talk about her. You never knew her. You can't possibly understand. You have both of your parents. They were there for your graduation from high school and college, and our wedding. Your mother knows our kids. She has a *relationship* with them. Don't talk to me right now! I don't even know if I can go to Mom's grave with Helen and Fiona. I don't know if I can face my aunt and uncle. They are counting on me. They are doing this *for* me, and I don't even know if I can go through with it. I'm so scared I can't even breathe."

I gasp for breath. Talking so fast made my head hurt. I breathe in and out for a moment, calming myself. "Deep down, I know I have to face this, Tom, but I feel like I'm on the flippin' Titanic, and water is everywhere...no matter what I do." I sit down at the kitchen table and lay my head down gently.

Tom walked over and put a steaming cup of joe in front of my face. He patted my head. "I know, I know. It's going to be okay. I know you need to talk about this, but you've got to hustle. We have to drop your car off this morning at the garage for your new tires. So, let's say we finish this conversation when I take you to work. I'll get the kids up. You shower because you reek of smoke and look like hell."

"Great," I say sarcastically, my head still on the table.

"I'm just trying to get things moving," Tom said as he walked up the stairs to wake the kids.

"I'm not moving," I replied. I heard Tom laughing upstairs.

"I didn't hear you!" He yelled sarcastically.

"I don't know how I can drink this coffee without leaving this position." I stared at the coffee longingly wanting to drink it but too lethargic to move my head.

I heard Tom upstairs talking with our kids, and I realized I had to go on this trip. I had to face my fears. It was time to grow up. I may have been sixteen when Mom died, but it was about time I stopped acting like a child and face my past. I know I can't keep drinking myself into a stupor and think it'll help me, especially when I have to deal with twenty-five five-year-olds for eight hours with a massive hangover. *How the hell am I going to get the aspirin out of the cabinet if I can't even lift my head to drink coffee?*

By the time I got to work, the coffee and aspirin had kicked in. Tom had literally talked me "off the ledge" and calmed me down. He further convinced me that going on the trip was the best decision. He kept saying, "It's a process to healing." I'm not sure what he meant by that, but it sounded good. I guess after so many years of dealing with me and my meltdowns, he's become pretty good at psychotherapy. I really don't know what I did to deserve him.

Work was work, but the bonus was I got to take my class to the third grade play of *The Titanic* of all things.

Anyway, as I watched the play and made sure the children were behaving, I was mentally making a list of all the things I had to do before I left town.

• Make sure there are plenty of groceries; easy dinners for Tom to prepare

- Laundry needs to be caught up and put in rooms
- Make list for Tom about where kids need to be and when
- Pack
- Find ride to the airport since Tom can't take me
- Um….

I was interrupted by, "Mrs. Moer! Mrs. Moer! I had an accident!" Little Bennett from my class was crying.

We've been in school for one hundred seventy-nine days, and the kids still call me the wrong name. Sometimes it is "Merlin," sometimes it's "Moer," but my all-time favorite is "Mrs. Moron." It's a good thing I have a sense of humor. "What's wrong, sweetheart?" I asked. I noticed he was holding the back of his bum.

"I ate too many raisins," he said as he cried harder.

I tried not to laugh and said, "Bennett, it happens to me all the time."

That sad little face broke into a smile from ear to ear once he heard that his beloved teacher poops her pants, too. I took his hand and waved to the other teacher to let her know I was leaving with a student. After an hour or so, we realized it wasn't the raisins after all. A bad case of diarrhea was hitting our class with a vengeance. *Perfect, just another fun day in kindergarten.*

Once school was out, I tried to multi-task as much as possible. I picked up my youngest son, Seth, and the rest of the neighborhood kids since it was my day for the carpool. I dropped Seth off at the house and ran to the grocery store. Once back home, I unloaded the groceries, and then put a Stouffer's Lasagna in the oven to cook while I headed upstairs to pack. My suitcase was open on the floor, and I was trying to fit whatever I could inside, knowing I had little time without distraction. I heard the phone ring but decided to let one of the kids answer.

"Mom, it's Aunt Helen on the phone." My daughter, Ginny, was standing in my doorway, arm stretched out, offering me the cordless phone.

I tripped over my suitcase reaching for it and just lay there, sprawled half in the bag, half out. "Hey, Helen." I sigh.

Helen doesn't miss a beat, though I know she heard the commotion on my end. "Megan, listen. I'm carrying my luggage on the plane tomorrow, and I need you to bring me some cute outfits in The Collection." The Collection is essentially all of the cute clothes that I pack for the trip. In the beginning, we thought we could just throw our things together and make outfits out of pieces from each person's closet. Let's be real, though. If there's one thing in this life I know, it is fashion. Helen is always pulled from one end of the earth to the other and doesn't pay attention to her clothes. She would rather feed and clothe her kids than herself. She may have three outfits, total, to her name. And Fiona spends most of her time in a tennis skirt or golf shorts. Those don't really go with my skirts and tops and dresses. So over the years, I've pretty much started packing for everyone.

We display The Collection in the closet of the hotel room. Shoes and accessories are also included. Anyone can wear anything in The Collection, on a "first come, first served" basis.

I laughed. "Helen, I've packed fifteen outfits for three days. We're good; just pack your underwear because you're not borrowing mine again."

Helen is notorious for never packing essentials when we go on our annual girls' trip. On our last trip, she forgot her underwear, and I never heard the end of her relentless ridicule of my oversized granny underwear. "So, I like it big and comfy. It's clean, and you really don't have any other options," I had retorted when teased.

Helen continued to ramble on the phone without taking a breath, "Colleen is at dance class until eight. Casey is at basketball practice, Mike had a cross-country meet, and Maggie is trying to find a backpack for me to use as a suitcase. I can't talk long, but I'll see you tomorrow at the baggage claim. Don't call me because Mike will have my phone. His cross-country meet is out of town, and he lost his phone, so I'm giving him mine first thing in the morning. Do you have my flight info?"

"Yep, it's printed and in my purse. Do *you* know your flight information?" I'm joking, but I am seriously wondering if she knows it, considering I made her flight reservations for her.

"Of course, I do." She responds indignantly.

"Okay, well you're supposed to arrive at nine-thirty at O'Hare, so Fiona and I will check the flight status on the road to Chicago."

"Good job, Maggie!" Helen yells.

"What?"

"Maggie just found me a book bag, so all I need now is some cute shoes that will flatter the many outfits from The Collection."

"Don't you and Colleen wear the same shoe size? Can you borrow some of hers?"

"Megan, I don't have time to tell you the story about Colleen and shoes but remind me tomorrow to tell you and Fiona. It's so her. Okay, I have to take this call because it's Tim. He's out of town, and I know he wants to know the details about Mike's meet. See you later, Megan."

"See you tomorrow, Helen."

"Bye."

I pull myself off the floor and toss the phone on the bed. I think to myself, *I can't wait to be with my sisters. I can't wait to lay awake in bed and talk until we fall asleep like we did as kids. I can't wait to be in their company and talk about nothing of importance. I can't wait to wake up in the morning and drink coffee without any interruptions. I can't wait to have a happy hour with them that actually lasts for hours, and we laugh until we can't breathe. I can't wait to be with my sisters!*

I am immediately pulled from my daydream by Ginny yelling at the top of her lungs from the office down the hall.

"Mom, it won't print, and Liam won't help me!"

"Okay, I'm coming!"

Ginny is our fourteen-year-old daughter. We named her for my mother. She is a ray of sunshine on a rainy day. Of course, only when she's in a good mood. When she's not, look out because sometimes her head starts to spin in a rage for absolutely no reason. Poor thing has hormones coming out of her ears and can't control any of them. She becomes exasperated at the drop of a hat. Now on a good day, when the stars are aligned just so and she's had her eleven hours of sleep, and her brothers haven't eaten all the pop tarts, she is the perfect daughter.

She's considerate, extremely sweet, and never meets a stranger. Ginny is very quick-witted and doesn't have a clue how beautiful she is. One of the things I love most about her is every day when she comes home from school, she walks over to the fridge, opens both doors, looks at the contents, and says, "Mom, how was your day?" She genuinely cares and that's something that can't be faked. So in the meantime, while her hormones are out of control and she's yelling at everybody, I know she doesn't mean it. I was once a teenager myself.

When I walked down the hallway, Seth was lying on his stomach with his feet crossed, his elbows bent, and the controllers in his hands moving a hundred miles per hour. The TV was on the floor about five inches from his face. He was yelling into his headset at his friend Russell, "I got you! I got you, Russell!"

Seth is twelve years old and our youngest. I can't imagine our lives without my little guy. Sometimes he puts his head in my lap when we're watching TV, so I'll scratch it. Maybe it's because he still has that cradle cap on his head, but he's like a little puppy dog always looking for someone to satisfy an itch for him. He's probably the most sensitive of all our kids, but that doesn't fool me. He's smart as a whip and very competitive. We call him the "Great White Hope." Mainly, we're hoping he will play high school sports. He may not be the most athletic kid on the team, but he is all heart. He is his father's clone.

"Seth, quit playing that stupid XBOX and clean your room. This place looks like a tornado hit it!"

"Mom, it's all Liam's stuff, I promise."

"Riiiiight…. Clean it up anyway. Tell Russell you have to go."

"Russell, I gotta go." He takes the headset off and starts picking up the dirty clothes littering the floor.

"Mom! Help me, please!" Ginny yells. "I hate this stupid printer! It never works when I need it to! Mom, this paper has to be turned in tomorrow, or I get a zero. Do you understand what I'm saying? It's the last day of school, and it has to be turned in or I *fail!*" Tears well in her eyes and begin to roll down her cheeks.

"Okay, let me look at this. Maybe it's not hooked up right." I fumble with the cords and have no idea what I'm doing. "Honey, Daddy is going to be home in about half an hour, and he can get this thing to work. Just go downstairs and eat dinner. We will take care of it later. It's okay, don't stress. Worst case, we can put the paper on a flash drive, and you can print it at school. Don't worry; it's going to be fine. You will not get a zero."

A voice floats up the stairs. "Hey, Mom! We have to go. We're going to be late."

Shit! I forgot I have to go with Liam to a college meeting at the high school. I give Ginny a hug and tell her again to eat dinner, and I yell the same to Seth as I'm running down the stairs. I grab my purse and head out the front door.

Liam is our oldest son. He's sixteen years old, smart, funny, and in love with his 1995 Chevy Tahoe. He works at the car wash on the weekends, which helped him purchase the car. He has all the qualities that I always wanted growing up. He's confident, good looking, and knows when to keep his mouth shut...a quality I'm still trying to perfect. He crams about fifteen minutes before his tests, and on a bad day, he earns a B. He has the power to achieve greatness, but sometimes is too lazy to realize it. Tom and I joke that he has alligator arms because his arms are too short to pull out his wallet and pay for things. Now that he's working, he understands the value of a dollar. "Nothing wrong with being frugal," I tell him all the time.

He has the keys in the ignition and the motor running. He's listening to The Red Hot Chili Peppers CD when I hop in. He flashes his million-dollar smile, and sings to me, "That's okay, we're late, but I don't need to go to college." He laughs, puts the car in reverse, and we head to the meeting. I just wish I could get him to care about his room like he does his car. *A mother's work is never done*, I think to myself.

When we arrive home two hours later, the dirty dishes from dinner are in the sink, Ginny is still complaining about the printer not working, and Seth is still playing XBOX.

"Where's your dad?" I ask.

"The cartridge needed to be replaced, so he went to Wal-Mart, but I think he was heading to the Windjammer," answers a frustrated Ginny. Perfect. I keep thinking, *Fourteen hours. Fourteen hours, and I will be heading to the airport and be free of responsibility.*

I cleaned the dishes, folded the laundry, and printed Ginny's paper at the neighbor's house. I was physically exhausted. I showered and got ready for bed in record time because trying to keep my eyes open actually hurt. I crawled into bed and pulled the covers over my shoulders, turned off the light, and relaxed. Maybe three minutes later the bedroom door opened, and I faintly heard my husband's voice in the background.

"Megan, are you asleep?"

I answered him with my eyes closed. "No, what's up?"

Now, Tom is my fourth child that just so happens to be my husband. He's a southern boy who is forty-seven but thinks he is twenty-seven. He owns five skateboards, three of which are long boards; five surf boards; two stand up paddle boards; and he has no idea what the word "sale" means. He shops by what he likes, not by what he can afford. He is the biggest kid in the family. Tom never says no to a beer or a trip to his favorite store, Charleston Watersports. He has more clothes than a sorority house, but he's our Tom, and we love him.

"Sorry about Ginny's paper. I went to three stores before I could find the right cartridge. I guess you guys got it printed? Considering it took a lot of time and effort to find the cartridge, I didn't want the night to be a total loss, so I met Neil and Ed at the Jammer for a couple of beers. I just wanted to make sure you were okay before you left tomorrow. Do you have a ride to the airport?"

I nod my head up and down because I am too tired to talk. "Amy is driving me," I say softly.

"I know this going to be tough on you and your sisters, but I have one request, Meg?"

"What's that?" I ask as I roll over on my side to get a better look at him.

"Do what you have to do. Whatever that is. Forgive yourself. Come back a happier person."

I look at him and whisper, "That's easier said than done."

"What time do you have to be at school in morning?"

"Meehan wants me there by seven. I'm exhausted. I need to go back to sleep now, okay?" I roll over on my stomach and pull my pillow towards me.

He leans over the bed and kisses my cheek. "I love you," he says softly, "I'm going to put the cartridge in the printer and watch TV downstairs for a while."

I mumbled "okay" through the pillow.

"Call me when you get to Fiona's tomorrow?"

"I will. Night, Tom. I love you."

"Night, Meg. Love you, too."

Chapter Two

Adios My Friend

"Reagin had a great year in kindergarten thanks to you," her mother said.

"Well thank you for being such a great Room Mom. We couldn't have survived this year without you. You were so great about contacting all the parents and organizing the classroom parties and big events."

"Glad to help," she replied. "Just remember Reagin's brother turns five this summer, so you make sure he is in your class in the fall!"

"Scouts promise," I say as I place my two fingers in the air. We both chuckle, and she walks away quickly, trying to catch up to her kids.

"Reagin, stop running!" She yelled as she ran after them.

"Have a great summer!"

"You too!" I yelled down the hall. I turned around and walked back into my classroom.

Mark, the school custodian, walks into my room about three minutes later. Mark is great with the kids. He usually decorates his office door for every holiday. As a matter of fact, we told the kindergartners a couple of years ago that we were going on a field trip to visit Mr. Mark's office on the other side of the school. He had two Christmas trees decorated, blinking lights all over his door, and a sign that said, "BEWARE OF THE GRINCH." A couple of snowmen were involved as well, but some of the older kids dismantled them.

"Moller, I'm heading over to the restaurant and wanted to make sure that there isn't anything else you need from me?"

"You have the Top Ten Reasons Why Meehan Shouldn't Retire list and the pictures, right?"

"Yes, ma'am, and all of the instructions with them. I can't believe you aren't going to be there."

"I know, but that's why you're in charge. You are going to be a great MC for the event. Please make sure somebody videotapes this for me. I hate that I'm going to miss the look on Meehan's face!"

"I think I'm going to drop the Oprah bit…."

"*What?* Mark, that's the best part of the whole skit. You have to! *Please* do the Oprah bit? Mrs. Umberger made the Oprah poster. It's going to be great. It's a perfect fit! Meehan will think she's the subject of your speech since she's dedicated her life to children for more than twenty-five years. She will be all ready to get up and take a bow, but then you'll pop out the poster of Oprah. It will be hilarious. You have to do it!" I said, pulling on his sleeve like a five year old trying to persuade him.

"All right, but if you're wrong you will pay, Moller!"

"I know…cupcakes and cookies from any future party we have in our classroom will be reserved just for you."

He laughed and gave me a high five. "Have a good trip, Moller. I'll see you in the fall."

Just as Mark was walking out of the room, Meehan walked in. "Megan, the paint center needs to be cleaned up and the block center needs to be covered with butcher paper," Mrs. Meehan said.

"Okay, let me know what else I need to do before I leave." I was cutting it close. My flight was leaving in two hours, and I still had to go home first.

"You know how Mrs. Smith is—she wants everything put away at the end of the year, so the cleaners can come in and wax the floors and clean the walls and the carpets."

"Right, right, right," I mumbled. "I mean seriously, it isn't like they clean this place any other day. That candy wrapper has been on the floor for three months now. I know this because I left it there," I said disgustedly.

"What are you talking about?" Meehan asked.

"Never mind," I said as I picked up the candy wrapper myself.

"She is very particular, especially at the end of the year," Meehan said.

"I know, but I couldn't get anything done with the parents in the classroom. They were all Chatty Cathys today. You would think that families would be running out of here to start their summer vacation on the last day of school."

"Of course not. They're afraid to spend time with their kids. They're probably thinking of how they can prolong the inevitable, and that's why they want to talk about nothing."

"Well, talking to Vinny's mom about his dad's new girlfriend really doesn't have anything to do with his end of the year report card."

"She talked to you about that, too?"

"I guess the new woman is also the new secretary at her ex-hubby's office, and things are starting to heat up between the two." I walked over to the paint center to start cleaning. "Okay, do you care if I throw away these half-used bottles of brown paint, or do you want me to leave them for the new teacher?"

I looked at Meehan because she didn't respond, and I noticed that she was crying. I tried to catch her off-guard. "I didn't think you were that attached to the brown?"

She attempted to laugh, but I knew what she was thinking. The woman's teaching career was ending after twenty-five years, and I wasn't going to be there to celebrate with her. It upset me that I wasn't going to be there for her special day, but it was unavoidable. We had planned our trip almost a year in advance. It was the only weekend we could all get away, the only time our aunts and uncles didn't have anything planned, and the only weekend I had off before I started my summer job.

What Meehan didn't know was that I planned a great surprise for her retirement luncheon. She was going to love the top ten list of reasons she shouldn't retire, as well as the pictures taken all over the school with other teachers and faculty. I had singers from previous classes who are now in high school coming to present her with flowers after performing a song I made up and reciting a funny poem about our years together.

The entire faculty helped out. We put a lot of time and effort into her retirement luncheon. Meehan and I had been a team for eight years: five days a week and eight hours a day. She was the Mutt to my Jeff, mainly because I'm five feet, nine inches, and she's a midget. I loved to make fun of her because she is petite, yet she has a black belt in karate. Despite her physical size, there is nothing little about this lady. Her personality is larger than life, and she knows how to take a joke.

Meehan became more than just a boss to me. We both were born and raised in Ohio, and she also has three kids, two boys and one girl. Family has always been a priority for both of us, and we love to drink red wine. Even though she is only eighteen years older, she became a mother to me in many ways. She has listened to my typical marital problems, given good advice about raising kids, and always encouraged me to make time for myself, which is easier said than done, but I love the idea.

Right before Christmas break in the fourth year we worked together, Meehan gave me a present. She said, "It's something that I don't use anymore, and I thought you might like it."

"Mrs. Meehan, you didn't have to give me anything! But you know, I do say it is always better to receive than to give," I said with a big smile on my face.

"Yeah, I don't think that's how the saying goes, but I thought you might put this to use."

Mary Meehan had been brought up in the Catholic Church, but for some reason, she didn't feel the connection anymore. She started attending a different church, but she knew the value of the rosary. She said, "I'm re-gifting, but I don't think you'll mind."

I opened the present and started to cry. Mary wasn't sure what was going on, and I couldn't control my emotions enough to tell her. She had given me a rosary made out of red roses. I don't think she realized the importance and value of her gift to me. Mary has always known that my mother died from cancer on Christmas Day when I was sixteen years old, but she didn't

23

know that my mother prayed novenas all the time. I was taught growing up that St. Theresa sends spontaneous flowers when prayers are heard. Mom prayed novenas constantly when she was sick. Every time she received flowers, she would burst into tears. That was her way of knowing her prayers were heard.

As I held the rosary in my hand, I couldn't find the words to tell Mary how it made me feel. She sat down, handed me a box of tissues, and waited patiently for me to compose myself. After about ten minutes, I told her that the rosary was the best present I had ever received from anyone.

Despite our deep friendship, I wasn't thinking about her journey as a teacher on this June day. I was thinking about the one I was about to embark on with my sisters. Selfishly, I was thinking of how I could get out of there and get to the airport to catch my flight. I knew I still had a lot of mental baggage that needed packing for this trip.

I said my last good-bye to my co-workers and got into my car. Everyone knew what to do for Meehan's retirement luncheon. Brenda was coordinating the singers, Linda was picking up the flowers, Jennie had the poem that I wrote, and Mark had the posters. Everything was going as planned except for the fact that my flight was now leaving in less than two hours, and I still had to go home first.

My best friend Amy, the guidance counselor at school, was taking me to the airport since Tom was working out of town. I pulled into the driveway and raced inside the house. I only had a couple of minutes to get ready before she arrived.

Chapter Three

The Letter

"Hello, Mommy's home!" I announced to my kids, as I walked in the house.

Liam, Ginny, and Seth were all watching TV in the family room.

"Really guys, this is your first day of summer vacation, and you're watching *Teen Mom*? Go to the pool or the beach for crying out loud."

"We are waiting to go to that stupid luncheon you volunteered us for today, Mom," Liam said.

"Oh yeah, sorry. Thank you so much for doing that. I know Meehan is going to love hearing you guys sing."

"I don't know the words to the song," Ginny said.

"Just hum loud, and nobody will know the difference," I tell her.

"Mom, when are you leaving?" Seth asks.

"As soon as Ms. Daniell picks me up. I've gotta grab my suitcase and wait for her outside." I drop my purse on the kitchen table and head for the stairs.

I ran upstairs to my room and looked in my closet. I debated taking my blue blazer. *Okay, I'm going to take it, but I have to take something out.* I pull everything out of my bag as I try to figure out my staple outfits for the weekend.

Downstairs I hear the kids yell, "Ms. Daniell is here!"

"Okay, tell her I'm coming," I yell downstairs.

"Mom, what's for lunch?" Ginny calls up.

Doesn't anybody listen to me? "Guys, I'm leaving," I yell back. "There's lunch meat in the fridge."

n we order a pizza?"

"Sure, get some money out of my purse. It's downstairs on the kitchen table."

I grabbed my suitcase and headed downstairs to kiss and hug the kids good-bye.

"I love you punks. Please be good for Dad. Thank you for singing for Meehan. I know she is going to love it!"

"Uh huh," says Liam

"Ginny, please answer the phone when I call okay? I want to hear your voice, so don't text me." Ginny had just gotten a new phone with a texting plan for her birthday and was obsessed with texting people.

"Yes, ma'am, but can I text you and give you updates on how the weekend is going?"

"Yes, but just answer when I call! I love you. Two kisses, right here," I point to my cheek.

Ginny stood on her toes to reach me.

I pointed to my other cheek, and Seth planted two kisses on me.

"Love you, Mom," he said.

"Liam, be good and help Dad if he needs it. I will see you on Monday night." He walked over and gave me two kisses on the cheek. He knows the drill. I don't even have to point to my face.

"Sing loud!" I yelled, hustling to the door with my suitcase and purse in tow.

"Ugh! Why are we doing this? I don't even know the song," Ginny complained.

I tripped over shoes in the entry way as I fought my way out the front door. I stopped. "Come on, guys. At least take these shoes out of here before someone breaks their neck."

"We will move them when it's time to go. We are wearing those shoes to the luncheon," Liam responded.

"Okay, good. I'm going to be late. Bye, guys. Be good!" I finally made it out the front door and towards the car.

Amy opened the back door of her car, so I could throw my luggage in.

"Thanks, buddy. Remind me to leave you a tip. This thing is so heavy, and I know I probably won't even wear half of the things I packed. I just hope I don't have to pay a fee because of the weight of this darn thing."

"Me, too, I know how cheap you are. Any fee will cut into your spending money."

"Yeah, and I don't have much to begin with."

I jumped in the front seat and fastened my seat belt.

"So what are the plans are for the next couple of days?" Amy asked as she backed out of my driveway.

"Well, right now I'm flying to Dayton, and Fiona is picking me up. From there she and I will drive to Chicago and pick up Helen and Suzanne at O'Hare Airport. Then we are all riding to Dubuque together. Helen will be flying in from West Palm Beach, Florida, and Suson is flying in a couple hours later from Richmond, Virginia. Once we get to Dubuque, we will meet up with my mom's relatives: her sister, my aunt Kitty; and her brother, my uncle John. We are planning to go to Mom's grave on Saturday, and then we will head home on Sunday. I'm staying with Fiona in Dayton for an extra day, and I will get to see my dad before I leave."

"Wow, that sounds like a busy schedule. Now who is Suson?"

"Suzanne (a.k.a Suson Fuson) and Helen met through their husbands' work when they were both living in Windsor, England. That was like nineteen years ago. She was like an older sister to Helen when they were together in England. Helen was pregnant for the first time with no family around, and Suzanne really took her under her wing.

"She had a couple of kids of her own and was there for Helen when we couldn't be since we were so far away. The first time I met Suson was at the Cincinnati Airport. I had no idea what she looked like, but I was supposed to meet her at her gate. She knew me before I knew her because she had seen pictures of me. We hit it off instantly! She truly has become one of us. She goes on every trip, and it doesn't matter where we go because we have so much fun with her. I don't know how she puts up with our silliness, but she does. Even though her name is Suzanne Fuson, we call her Suson Fuson."

"Gotcha. So when was the last time you were at your mom's grave?" Amy asked as she looked straight ahead, her hands at the ten o'clock and two o'clock positions on the wheel.

"About fourteen years ago. All six of us kids went out with our spouses and children one Christmas. Ginny was about six months old, and Liam was two. We drove the twelve hours to Dayton where we met up with all three of my brothers, both of my sisters, and all of their spouses and kids. We stayed there for the night. Then, the next day we loaded up and drove the eight hours from Dayton to Dubuque. The weather was terrible; can you believe that?" I laughed as I said it. "Snow, wind, and freezing ice all over the highways; it got scary driving because only one lane was open, and I think we were the only people crazy enough to be out on the roads. We had six cars following each other very carefully through the snow. It was like our own parade. We went out to see my cousin who was sick with breast cancer and living in Cedar Rapids. It was a tough trip because we basically went out to say good-bye to her and stop by Mom's grave. Even though it was hard going out there with the weather and all and seeing my cousin, we were so glad we did because she died shortly after that. That was my aunt Kitty's daughter, Sarah Beth."

Amy listened attentively, which is usually what she does when I talk. She always lets me speak my mind no matter how boring I am or how many times she has already heard the story or how insignificant it might be. She's such a good friend to me. I guess that's one of the bonuses of having a friend that's a counselor.

The first time I met Amy was when I was having trouble with a student and had to take him to her office. She had been working at the school for two weeks, but I hadn't introduced myself yet. When I knocked on her door, she finished up a phone call and waved us in.

"Hi, what can I do for you guys?" She was energetic and eager to help, but what stood out to me was her mason jar of Skittles that read Bully Beans. The funny thing about it was that it was already half empty.

"Ms. Daniell, I wasn't aware that there was so much bullying going on here at school? Your bully bean jar seems kind of low, doesn't it?"

She laughed. "I know, but the good news is that I think we've figured it out…apparently Mr. Mark is being harassed by the lunch ladies."

We both started laughing and became fast friends. From that day on, we felt comfortable talking to each other about everything.

I looked out the passenger side window and thought about my mom.

"I can't believe she's been gone for twenty-five years. There is so much I remember, but so much I would like to forget."

"I know. If there's anyone who understands what you mean, it's me." She says sincerely. I know she's right.

Amy pulls the car into the departures drop off lane. "Here we are at the Charleston Airport, and you have twenty-seven minutes to spare. Just enough time to be frisked inappropriately by security and still enjoy a cold beer."

"Thanks for the ride. Let me know how the luncheon goes, okay?" I wrestle my suitcase out of the back seat.

"Will do! I will call as soon as it's over, good or bad, but I know it will be great! Good luck. Call me if you need to talk."

"Thanks again for the ride. I really appreciate it so much."

I walked into the airport and waited in the ticket line since the Kiosk machines weren't working. The temperature was extremely hot, even for Charleston in June. The humidity was so thick that I could cut it with a knife. As I waited in the line, I thought about a career change.

Maybe I should be a weatherman? Living in Charleston would be a cakewalk. How easy would it be to predict the weather? "Gonna be another hot one today folks." I mean, throw in a small percentage of rain every day, and boom! The forecast is done.

"Can I help you?" I pulled out of my daydream as the ticket agent asked for my photo I.D. With a couple of clicks on the computer and some pleasantries, she produced my boarding pass. Security was quick, and I reached my gate in record time. I decided to have that cold beer since the drinking establishment was next to my departure gate. *Things are working out! I like this!*

I strolled to the bar and ordered a Guinness. I put my purse on the bar and rested my weary body, letting out a deep sigh of relief that I actually had time to spare. Looking around, I noticed other travelers and wondered what their stories were. *Where are they going and who are they going to see? Are they traveling on business or pleasure?* My thoughts were interrupted by the bartender placing a napkin down and putting my beer on top.

"Thanks," I said and smiled.

"You're welcome. Where are you traveling today?"

"I'm headed to Dayton, Ohio now, and then driving on to Dubuque, Iowa with my sisters."

"So a girls' trip, huh?"

"Yep, a sisters' trip. We do it every year." I took a sip of my beer.

"I guess the sisters' trips to the Bahamas or South Beach are totally overdone. Sure, I get it. The mid-west is really cool," the bartender replied as he wiped down the counter with a sarcastic look on his face.

I laughed at his comment. "I know it does sound a bit strange. We are going to see my mom's side of the family. My sisters and I all live in different cities, and we haven't seen these relatives in a long time. It just seemed like the thing to do this year."

"Well, that's cool. Let me know if you need anything," he said and walked to the end of the bar to take a drink order.

I took another sip of my beer and felt the release of not having to take care of anyone for three days. *I am officially on break from my family.* I sighed in relief. I leaned back, placed my feet on top of my suitcase, and started to play with my phone when I noticed a yellow envelope sticking out of my purse. For some reason, I didn't take it out immediately to look at it. Instead, I just stared at it and wondered why it was there. *Where did that thing come from?* I wasn't sure how I didn't see it before, but there it was, looking right at me. I opened the envelope and started to read a typed letter.

Dear Megan,

I have been thinking about writing this to you for a couple of weeks now because I know how hard this trip will be for you and your sisters. I want you to know that you are a true and dear friend to me. I feel like we share so much in our lives, trying to raise decent children in this crazy world. We have also both suffered a great deal of pain and loss in our lives. I have so many unanswered questions, but I do know that your mom and my brother are probably the reason we met each other. They knew that you and I were a perfect fit when it came to friends.

Sometimes I let my imagination get the best of me, but I have my ideas about heaven. I think that it is like a big football field, and they are all up there watching us fail and succeed. But your mom and my brother are the ones that are cheering us on. Your mom is saying, "That's my daughter. She's the one with the curly hair. God puts her in place when people are at their worst, and she makes it better. She is God's secret weapon. I'm so proud of her."

You're a great mother and friend, and I know in my heart that your mother loves you very much.

Thanks for being my friend.

Amy

Amy's words were exactly what I had always wanted my mother to say to me. When my mother was alive, I never did anything to make her proud of me. As a result, I have spent most of my adult life dreaming of meeting her and hearing her say those words. My husband and I often argue about my inability to say "no" to people (except to him, of course). I guess it is because I don't want to disappoint anyone. I know I did a lot of that as a kid, so I've spent the rest of my life trying to make up for it. In addition to a couple of Hail Marys and Our Fathers on a daily basis, I'm basically serving a penance of always saying "yes" to anyone who needs something from me. I have carried so much guilt for as long as I can remember. Not for anything I did, but for what I *didn't* do when my mother was sick. I think to myself, *I'm tired of feeling inadequate and unworthy. It has to end.*

Amy must have slipped the envelope in my purse on the way to the airport. I want to call her and thank her, but I can't let go of the letter. I continue to re-read her words, "Your mother loves you." My heart is smiling as I read them.

I always wonder what she would think of me if she met me today. *Would she like me? Would she think I am good enough? Does she forgive me for not doing more for her and our family when she was sick? Does she forgive me for not taking better care of my little sister? What would she think of her grandchildren? Does she think I'm a good mother?* I will never be able to ask her those questions, but I don't know how to move forward and accept the card that has been dealt. After twenty-five years, I'm still so angry. I feel cheated from a lifetime of memories with my mother. I need to understand why her life had to end when it did, but I don't believe I ever will.

I took another sip of my beer and heard over the loud speaker, "Last call for flight 1242 to Dayton."

The bartender turns to me and says, "I think they're calling you. Your beer is on me. Have fun with your sisters."

I give the best smile I can with my mouth closed and wipe my tears as I put the letter in my purse. "Thanks," I say. I pull out a couple of bucks and put them on the bar for a tip. I grab my suitcase and throw my purse over my shoulder as I walk toward the gate to board flight 1242 to Dayton.

Chapter Four

August 1985: The Teams

"Caroline, I don't think he even knows my name, and he's dating that Beth girl that just graduated last spring. Why are we doing this?" I whined.

"I want to talk to Doug Knoll, and Jimmy Dunne is over there with him. Neither of us have good prospects for homecoming. Let's pretend we haven't gotten our pictures taken yet and just walk by them and start up some conversation. Just follow my lead," Caroline prodded.

It was the week before school started and picture day for the fall sports program, which was passed out at every home football game. The parking lot of the high school was packed with cross country runners, football players, cheerleaders, and boys and girls soccer teams. It was a mini reunion for kids to catch up with friends they hadn't seen all summer. Caroline and I were doubles partners on the Varsity tennis team and best friends to boot. She was a senior, and I was a junior at Cardinal Newman High School in Dayton, Ohio. We met on the elementary bus six years earlier. I informed her that she was sitting in the fifth grade area, and she needed to move accordingly to the sixth grade seats, which happened to be the row behind me. She had coke bottle glasses, baby fine blond hair, and braces that couldn't hide the friendliest smile. Caroline and I became best friends instantly.

Caroline lived three blocks from my house, and during the summer months, we worked at our neighborhood pool. She was a lifeguard because she was a fish in the water and passed the certification test. I, on the other hand, worked in the snack bar because I almost drowned taking the test. Not cool, but I did get to eat an endless supply of gummy worms and ice cream bars. Let's not forget to mention that I saved years on my skin since I was inside the snack bar instead of on the lifeguard stand.

Working in the snack bar really wasn't that bad of a job except for the adult swim break, which was the last fifteen minutes of every hour. Only the adults were allowed to swim in the pool while the lifeguards switched their posts. When that time came, about thirty-five dripping-wet kids bombarded the snack zone, pulling out their soggy dollar bills and coins and yelling out their orders all at once. To top it off, none of them knew how to count money.

If we weren't working, we would spend the day at the pool with all the other kids in the neighborhood. We would bring our tennis racquets and hit a couple of balls on the tennis courts once we got tired of swimming. The funny thing was, most days we would hit the ball maybe six times, and then lay out on the court the rest of the time. Some of our deepest talks took place on the tennis court with our backs on the ground looking up at the sky with our eyes closed, trying to get a tan. My mom's cancer, Jimmy Dunne, Doug Knoll, and Caroline's infamous checklist were all frequent topics. Caroline's father was a colonel in the Air Force and was very strict. Caroline, like most teenagers, lost her belongings on a regular basis and was not able to keep track of her things. Therefore, her dad made her keep a list with her at all times about what she was taking from the house when she left. Upon her arrival back home, she had to check the list and make sure she returned with everything she had when she left. One day when she was at my house, we were making fun of her list and how it wasn't necessary. We had decided that her parents were total control freaks. So I mocked her parents and the checklist.

"Caroline, let me see your list. Do you have your glasses? Check. Do you have your tennis racquet? Check. Do you have the tennis can? Check. Do you have all three balls in the tennis can? Check. House keys?"

"Yes, Mummy dearest," Caroline replied in a goofy voice. We laughed and said our good-byes, and she headed out the back door to cut through the yards to her house. My doorbell rang a few minutes later, and as I went to answer it, I noticed Caroline's bike parked in my driveway. I ran to the back door, slid open the screen, and yelled at the top of my lungs, "Caroline, you forgot your bike!" At that point, I realized that we needed to succumb to the list because maybe her dad wasn't that stupid after all.

So on that day in August 1985, I followed Caroline's lead, and we sauntered up to Jimmy Dunne and Doug Knoll who were on the Varsity soccer team at our high school. These guys were star athletes, very popular and cool—everything Caroline and I were not. I realized at this point that I was completely out of my league, but I couldn't run away because it would draw more attention to me. I didn't want any attention at all, so I just followed Caroline's lead and tried to blend in with the fence.

Caroline talked to Doug, and I pretended like I was straightening the strings on my tennis racquet when out of the blue, Jimmy Dunne asked me a question about tennis. I looked up at him and saw that he was smiling at me. Suddenly, I could feel heat burning my cheeks.

My stomach was in knots. Not only was I surprised that he knew who I was, but the way he looked at me made me feel like he was flirting with me. I smiled at him and immediately looked behind me. Thankfully, I didn't see anyone. I didn't answer his question either, though. Not because I didn't want to, but because I had no idea what he had asked me. I was in a tizzy just being in his presence. I just kept smiling. We looked at each other and just smiled for the next couple of minutes. I heard Caroline say good-bye to Doug, so I said good-bye to Jim. We walked to the car with our tennis racquets. When we closed the doors of the car, I screamed at the top of my lungs, "I'm such an idiot!" We both started laughing. I told Caroline that I froze and couldn't even answer his question and how I turned around thinking he was smiling at somebody else.

"I didn't notice anything. You were fine," she insisted.

She turned the radio on as we were leaving the school parking lot, and Tears for Fears blared out of the speakers, singing their popular hit, "Everybody Wants to Rule the World." We both sang at the top of our lungs and drove directly to G.D. Ritzy's ice cream shop, where we ordered Chunky Dory Fudge and talked about our potential homecoming dates. We had already learned the secret that ice cream and chocolate will always be a girl's best friend when contemplating deep thoughts about love and life, or better yet, one's future love life.

Caroline and I loved being doubles partners on the tennis team because we were always in the same frame of mind. We didn't care if we won or lost, and we really didn't care what our record was for the season. Our goal was to have fun, on and off the court. Most of the time, we goofed off and drove our coach crazy. Poor Mr. Painter had no idea what he was in for when he agreed to coach us my junior year. He had coached wrestling for seventeen years and decided that he was ready for a change, but I'm not sure Caroline and I were what he had in mind. I'm also not sure that going from an aggressive male sport to flighty hormonal girls was a good change either.

But what did I know? I was busy practicing my Russian accent because we pretended I was a foreign exchange student. Sometimes during the match I would yell something pretending to be Russian, and Caroline would laugh and miss the ball. My strategy was for the other team to miss the ball, but once she got the giggles, she couldn't stop laughing. It was hard to keep up the accent, and it hurt the back of my throat when I would yell words that started with the letter "c." So during the match I would take a break and drop the accent, but I would forget what I was doing. Caroline would notice the missing accent and say something, and we would both laugh uncontrollably. You could see the girls on the other side of the net talking to each other and feeling like idiots.

Mr. Painter would get so frustrated with Caroline and me because I think he thought we really could have been good tennis players if we had taken it seriously. But if there weren't any cute boys or fun snacks, we really weren't interested in winning. It just took way too much energy. Our focus was the Homecoming dance. One day during a match, I asked her right in the middle of a point if she had found an outfit yet for the dance. It broke my heart when she said, "My mom and I looked, but we haven't found anything yet." I guess I was jealous because she could go shopping with her mom, and I couldn't. Her mom would have helped me if I had asked, but I didn't want her help. I wanted *my* mom, and I knew that wasn't an option.

Whenever I needed an outfit or a dress, my mom was on a mission. We'd go to the Jo-Ann Fabric and Craft Store in Dayton and spend hours looking at the designs and patterns for the perfect outfit. I'd joke with her as I turned the pages of the books and fantasize that we were putting together the spring collection of a fashion magazine. She would just laugh and tell me to focus. After we chose the pattern, I would run my hands through the endless aisles of fabric and pick out the softest one. Mom would deliberate which colors looked best with my skin, which patterns were too busy, and of course, which one was the most economical. Mom was always frugal.

We had always talked about the dress she would make me when it was time for me to go to the Homecoming dance. Now that the time was here, I was even more conscious of how important my dress was. In one of my mom's incredible creations, I was sure to stand out. I had never thought about what I would do if she couldn't make my dress. Picking out a dress from Sears just wouldn't be the same.

Within two weeks of our initial non-conversation, Jimmy Dunne had asked me out. My mom was in the hospital at that time, and she had forbidden me from going out with any boy unless she met him first. So we went to the hospital together. When we walked into her hospital room, my dad was sitting next to her bed in a chair and my mom was reading a book. She smiled when she saw us, but you could tell she was hesitant to pass any kind of judgment on my new friend. Mom took off her bifocals, gave Jimmy a once over, and began her interrogation. She asked about the sports he played, what kind of grades he earned, how many people were in his family, and about his father's occupation. When she was satisfied with his answers, she then inquired about where we were going that afternoon. That, apparently, was the green light for us to go out.

We were going to a cookout with a bunch of kids, and I mentioned that "Sweet Caroline" was going to be there, too. Even now, I sometimes think that my mom loved Caroline more than she loved me. She smiled when I mentioned Caroline's name. She said for us to have a good time and not to be late. I gave her a hug and two kisses on her cheek, relieved the inquisition was over because I had suffered enough embarrassment for a lifetime. Jimmy said good-bye to both of my parents. As we turned to walk out, my mother called after us, *"No* drinking, you hear me?"

I was so embarrassed. Jimmy was extremely respectful and said, "Just a cookout, Mrs. O'Malley. There will be no drinking." I was a year and half younger than Jim, but I felt like I was five years old. I wanted to fade into the wall and disappear, but Jimmy must have known what I was feeling because he instantly took my hand and smiled at me. He waved to my parents with his other hand, and we walked out the door.

Over the next couple of months, Jimmy became the perfect boyfriend. He would write me poems, meet me outside of my classes to walk me to my locker, and surprise me with flowers. I don't think anyone has ever made me feel as special as he did. I was consumed with him. I became an avid soccer fan and went to all of the Varsity games, spent a lot more time in the bathroom getting ready for school in the morning, and constantly stared at him (without him knowing, of course) while he ate his lunch. He became my reason for everything. He eventually broke up with his college girlfriend, and we dated exclusively.

On Friday nights, we would meet at the football games and sit together with all of his friends, including Doug Knoll and Caroline, and then Saturday night would be date night.

We would go see a movie, meet friends, or just hang out at his house. My house was a depressing place to be, so I wanted to be anywhere but there. My dad would come home from the hospital after visiting my mom, and he and Fiona would watch *The Dukes of Hazard* and *Dallas*. They only kept the light next to the sofa in the family room turned on. The only other lights in the house were the flickering lights from the television.

My day-to-day existence consisted of Jimmy, tennis, work, and school. Friends from church set me up with a great job at a Hallmark store that was five minutes from my house. It was a perfect job if you liked to work alone and interact with very few people. I worked four-hour shifts and only saw about two people the whole time. Meanwhile, I would graze through the aisles and search for the perfect card for my Grandpa Delany. Grandpa Frank Delany was my mom's dad, and he lived in Dubuque, Iowa, which meant that we didn't see him very often. Every day, I would send him a card from work and write him a cute note. I also picked out my graduation party invitations, an event that was sixteen months away at the time. With all the studying I hadn't been doing, saying that I was optimistic was an understatement. I hunted through the "romantic" and "just for you" sections with Jimmy in mind but never really found anything that didn't seem too quirky. So I usually settled on the *Far Side* cards. Those were always my favorite. "Bob encumbered with a low self-esteem takes a job as a speed bump." That Gary Larson knew my kind of humor.

Homecoming weekend finally arrived, and I was ecstatic about my date and the dance to say the least. I was on the Homecoming Court and had about two hours before I had to be at school for the annual parade that was held before the game on Friday afternoon. I found out that my brother Shamus was home from school, and he was visiting Mom at the hospital. I jumped in my car, which was my mom's '76 Chevy Station Wagon, and headed down there to meet him. When I walked into her room at Miami Valley Hospital on September 19, you couldn't tell what color the walls were because cards and pictures were everywhere. It was her birthday. All three open walls were covered with sweet messages of well wishes from just about everyone in town. Bouquets of flowers decorated every table in the room, and birthday balloons were dancing on the ceiling. Yet, her own daughter who worked at a Hallmark store didn't have anything for her on her birthday. Ironically, in all the time I spent looking at cards for everyone else, I forgot about my mother's birthday. *How could I have forgotten?* I felt terrible. *Who does that?* My stomach sank, and my heart rate began to race. That moment was the first time I realized that my head and heart weren't in the same place.

I walked over to her bed and gave my mom a kiss. "Happy Birthday," I managed to say without crying. I had a huge lump in my throat, and I knew I wouldn't be able to hold it in. Shamus was telling Mom a story, and she was laughing so hard she was crying. He could always make her laugh. It was his ace in the hole. After he finished, he moved so I could sit beside her. "Mom, I'm getting a soda from Mrs. Skowren. Do you want anything?" He asked as he walked toward the door.

"No, I'm fine, honey," Mom replied.

"Okay, I will be back in a couple of minutes." With that, he walked out of the room and left us to talk.

"I'm so sorry, Mom. I don't have anything for your birthday." I felt deflated and began to cry. Mom put her arms around me and pulled me closer to her. She said, "Just you being here makes this day special. You could have gone to that football game and forgotten all about me, but you didn't."

She then asked me about my dress for the dance, but when I answered, she looked away from me. I followed her stare; she was looking at the doorway. A man stood there. He was of Indian descent and maybe five feet tall. He was wearing a long white coat with a stethoscope around his neck. He clearly had no interest in my mother as a human being; to him, she was only a chart. He walked into the room and announced in broken English that they had found spots on her brain.

She stopped him abruptly. "Please talk to my husband. I don't want to hear this. Please just talk to my husband." I watched my mom shake her head, and then I heard him again. The doctor spoke in his thick accent and repeated that they had found spots on my mother's brain.

What is he doing? I thought to myself. I couldn't believe that he was talking to Mom from the doorway and telling her that she now had brain cancer. Didn't he understand what she was saying to him?

"Please leave now," my mom told the doctor. "I'm talking with my daughter. Please call and talk to my husband." The doctor seemed agitated, but he turned around and left the doorway of her hospital room. I looked at Mom. She didn't say anything, but she bit the corner of her lip and stared at the doorway. Her thoughts were a million miles away. I couldn't say or do anything to make her feel better. I wanted to punch that egotistical doctor and tell him to learn some bedside manners. Instead, I leaned in and put my arms around her and rested my face on her cheek. She never cried, but I think it was because I was there.

"Megan, you probably have to get going. What time is the parade?" She asked. I looked at the clock in the room and realized I had about thirty minutes before I had to be back at school. "You're right. I do need to go, Mom. Are you going to be okay?"

"I'm fine. Shamus should be back any minute. He just went to grab that soda. You go ahead and have fun tonight. Tell your daddy to take pictures for me."

I gave my Mom a hug, and she pointed to her cheek. I kissed it two times, said "Happy Birthday," and walked out of her room. The walk to the elevator was like a dream. I found it hard to move my legs. I was in a fog. I heard the muffled sounds of people talking, but I couldn't make out what they were saying. I kept thinking about what I had just witnessed.

There's more cancer. She has spots on her brain. The cancer is spreading, and the treatments aren't working. Why is this happening to us?

As I stood in the elevator, I thought about how Mom and Dad worked as a team. He was the coach that gave encouragement and protected Mom as much as he could from any kind of negative news. She was the player that listened to him and grew from his strength. He only wanted her to focus on getting better and to keep a positive attitude. I knew they were both amazing, and I was lucky to be their daughter. I hoped I could make them as proud of me one day as I was of them.

Chapter Five

Welcome Home

M om came home from the hospital accompanied by three nurses, two EMS drivers, and one hospice nurse who escorted her into her new private room: the basement. My grandpa Delany and aunt Kitty came in from Iowa to make sure everything went smoothly. Aunt Kitty actually paid more attention to us kids than my mom that day; she was worried about us since Dad had been cooking our meals for the last four months while Mom had been in the hospital. Now, when I say meals, I mean a main entrée with no side dishes. When Dad cooked steak for dinner, it was just steak. No baked potato dripping with butter or sour cream, no salad, and definitely no dessert. The saying "you don't know what you have until it's gone" is true. Times had changed when my mom got sick and not for the better.

My mother was first diagnosed with cancer when I was fourteen. She developed a rare muscle cancer from melanoma on her back. She was in and out of the hospital for two years, during which time she suffered a stroke and the cancer spread to her lungs. She endured countless surgeries, hours of chemo, and the removal of her left lung. Her stroke left her paralyzed. For months, she was in physical therapy learning basic things all over again like eating, swallowing, and talking.

I missed many things about my mother while she was in the hospital. Her absence was a constant reminder that my world was not what it should be. I missed the smell of her perfume and the smell of her lasagna coming out of the oven. I missed having freshly washed linens on my bed. I would often sneak in her room just to stand in her closet and run my hands over her clothes, wishing things were different.

We all had specific jobs during Mom's extended hospital stays. Although there are six kids in our family, only three of us lived at home: Fiona, my big brother Murphy, and me. Murphy was in charge of carpool for Fiona. He took her to and from school every day, to basketball practice, and to play dates with friends. He was working and going to school full-time, and suddenly full-time nanny was part of his daily routine, too.

I was in charge of the household laundry. *Laundry?* I was sixteen years old, and the only laundry I did was carrying it from the laundry room back to my room after Mom had picked it up from my floor, washed and folded it, and placed it in my own personal pile. Even though I loved my clothes, I wasn't even sure which one was the washer and which was the dryer, much less if anything needed to be dry-cleaned. So, when I was told this was my responsibility, I did what any teenager would do: I hid the dirty laundry. I found a corner in the laundry room behind the air vent and started putting all of the dirty clothes that needed to be washed in that area. My plan was perfect, until we ran out of things to wear. Obviously, I didn't think that through. My dad began complaining about never having any clean shirts or underwear, and he finally asked me about it. "I've bought more undershirts and underwear in the last couple of months…." He continued on, but I found some reason to leave the room. "I don't get it," his voice trailed behind me.

Cleaning the house also became my responsibility, but for some reason, I could handle that chore. Just as long as I didn't have to change the sheets, things were good. Pine Sol became my new best friend: Pour a cup in each toilet, swirl it around, and let the smell transform the house. Vacuuming was easy, too; just making the marks in the carpet in a perfect formation made it look and smell like I had been cleaning for hours. I hate to admit that before my mother got sick, I had never lifted a finger to clean the house.

My older sister Helen was attending college downtown at the University of Dayton. Her college life was busy, but she knew what was important. Since the hospital was about six miles from where she lived, and she didn't have a car, she improvised. Helen would ask her roommates to drive her, and they would all go visit Mom. Sometimes they even roller-skated to the hospital.

Helen would come home almost every Saturday and pick up Fiona for the day. She would take her out to lunch or just let her hang out at her house with her roommates. Little Fiona was unofficially adopted by all of Helen's friends. Her immediate family grew by ten older sisters.

My brother Shamus was also in college, but he was attending Miami University in Oxford, Ohio. He tried to get home as much as he could during Mom's stay at the hospital, but when you don't have a car or money, traveling becomes more challenging. He said that when he needed a ride home for Mom's birthday, he made a poster that read: "Mom has 10 days to live. Need a ride to Dayton." When he didn't catch a ride, he decided to cross off the ten and make it a nine. When that didn't work either, he changed the number of days to eight, and so on. He said by the time he got down to six days, three cars pulled up at the same time. He weighed his options and made his decision by which car had the best AC, tunes, and snacks for the ride. We know it's not true, but it made a funny story.

So all of us lived in Ohio, except for my oldest brother Jack. He had just married his high school sweetheart and was in law school down in Austin, Texas, when Mom got sick. He and his wife Nancy were coming home for Christmas, and we couldn't wait to see them.

My dad's sister came to help us welcome my mom home from the hospital. She lived in Lewis County, Kentucky where she was a Dominican Nun. Sister Pat was great at saying the rosary, singing, and making us laugh, but cooking and cleaning… not so much.

Dad had ordered a hospital bed for my mom, and we set everything up for her downstairs in the basement. The area was open and light, and it was easy for everyone to maneuver around the bed. The bathroom downstairs was also handicapped-accessible, which was a main factor in moving her there. Sue, the hospice nurse, hooked up the oxygen machine and helped the nurses with the necessary paperwork. It was like a three ring circus, and Mom was the main event.

Nurse One showed my grandpa and Aunt Kitty exercises that Mom needed to do daily. Nurse Two talked to my dad about medication and diet. Nurse Three was Mrs. Skowren. She was a family friend who worked at the hospital. She talked to Mom, took her pulse, and tried to make her as comfortable as possible.

My parents had played bridge with Mr. and Mrs. Skowren, and their kids had grown up with us. Mrs. Skowren worked at St. Elizabeth's Hospital where Mom had been for the last four months, rehabilitating from her stroke. Her smiling face behind the nurses' station at the hospital was always comforting, and she tried to make our visits easier by offering sodas or bringing us snacks.

Mrs. Skowren came upstairs from the basement. I was in the hallway and greeted her with a hug. "Hi, Mrs. Skowren."

"Hi, Megan. How are you doing?"

"Good. I'm glad Mom is home. I just want her to get better, so things can get back to normal."

"Megan, we need to talk. Do you have a couple of minutes?"

"Sure."

We walked into the living room. She noticed our Charlie Brown Christmas tree and smiled. "Nice tree," she said.

"Thanks. It's about twenty-three years old," I announced proudly. "I know it looks terrible, but it's our tradition. We think it really represents our family."

"How?"

"It looks old and worn, but it still serves its purpose. Kind of like our spirit. It's beaten, but we're still standing. You know? Dad didn't want to put it up this year, but Fiona and I insisted on it."

"I like that tree more now than when I first saw it, Megan."
We both smiled. "It's got a lot of character," she said. "Do you all
need any help with Christmas shopping?"

"We went last weekend. Dad took us to Sears and told us
we had twenty minutes to bring back whatever it was we
wanted for Christmas. I'm getting a basketball and volleyball
net this year from Mom and Dad. Fiona's getting a fishing pole
and tackle box."

"I'm impressed you girls are so into the outdoors?"

"Actually, we were in the sporting goods section and didn't
have time to make it to the junior department on the fourth floor."

We both laughed and looked at the Christmas tree with the
obvious packages wrapped neatly under it.

"Megan, I'm going to get to the point because they're going to
be coming upstairs, and I want you to hear this before I go."

I looked at her, not knowing what she was going to say.

"Megan, I never got a chance to say good-bye to my mother
before she died. I never got to tell her thank you for everything
she had done for me." She paused, a tear rolling down her face.
"You have an opportunity to tell your mom good-bye. Take
advantage of this time, Megan, because you don't want any
regrets." She walked over and gave me a hug.

I tried to process what she had said as she left the room. The
other nurses and EMS drivers were coming up the stairs. The
drivers carried the gurney out the front door. Nurse Two talked
with my dad one last time, and she motioned for Mrs. Skowren.
He thanked them, opened the front door, and said good-bye. He
walked back downstairs to join my Mom and everyone else.

I was still sitting there alone with my thoughts, looking
at the Christmas tree, thinking about what Mrs. Skowren
had said. *Good-bye?*

Chapter Six

Merry Christmas

J ust four days after her homecoming, Mom was half the person she was when she had arrived. Her health had deteriorated tremendously, and things were getting worse. Her breathing was slower, and she was on full oxygen. She was incontinent and no longer eating. She could barely talk without losing her breath, but she was always asking about Jack. Murphy, Helen, Fiona, Shamus, and I had been with her constantly, but Jack, on his way home with Nancy, did not know what to expect. During those couple of days the house was busy with visitors. It was like a Wal-Mart on Black Friday. Teachers, relatives, neighbors, and family friends all brought coffee cakes and chicken casseroles.

Monday evening, Jack and Nancy arrived home. Jack gently kissed Mom on her forehead and said, "Mom, we're here." She slowly opened her eyes and sighed in relief, "Jack." She motioned for him to kiss her cheek. Mom then closed her eyes and slowly slipped into a coma, never to regain consciousness again.

We went to Christmas Eve Mass at St. Luke's Church. I remember sitting on the left side of the church behind the McGill family. I thought to myself, *It is so sad their father died around Christmas last year. It must be tough to lose someone at this time of year.*

I couldn't stop staring at them during the mass. *Are they reminded every Christmas of the loss they experienced?* When Mass was over, we walked to the car, and the cold wind blew on my face and made me snap out of my thoughts. We waited in the car for a long time for my dad because he was talking to so many people. I'm sure they were asking about my mom.

When we got home, we all went downstairs. Jack and Nancy had stayed behind to take care of Mom. They planned to go to midnight mass later that evening. I saw my sister-in-law, Nancy wiping Mom's head. Jack was talking to the two nurses that had just arrived at the house. One was from hospice and the other worked for the hospital.

It was a Christmas Eve unlike any other at the O'Malley house. We weren't eating Mom's cookies that she had slaved over for months. She always hid them in the freezer downstairs, wrapped in wax paper and stored in shirt boxes because she didn't own any Tupperware. No one was shopping for last minute Christmas gifts to be opened on Christmas Day or sitting by the Christmas tree looking at the lights. Instead, we were downstairs around Mom's bed, watching her breathe with extreme effort and praying for a miracle.

Christmas morning arrived, and we ran back and forth from the family room to the basement for most of the day. Dad had just gotten a VHS player for work, and we had rented the Karate Kid video, so we watched it a couple of times that day. We'd watch a little bit, pause it, and then go down and see Mom. Dad was busy in the kitchen cooking Christmas dinner. He made turkey, stuffing, mashed potatoes, and green beans. The most impressive part was the apple pie he made from scratch for dessert. The top of it even had the lattice that I'd only seen in magazines.

When we sat down for dinner in the dining room, we were all pretty amazed. Dad tried to keep the mood light, and Shamus made fun of his stuffing, saying it was giving him cotton mouth. I wanted to be a part of the banter and piped up, "Dad, Mom would just *die* if she saw how hard you worked and how great this all looks, I mean come on, especially the pie!"

I smiled, thinking I had given him a compliment, but the room became instantly quiet. Everyone looked at me in horror.

Why did I say that? Again, my head and heart were obviously not in the same place.

Shamus made some silly comment and tried to take the focus off of my stupidity. Dad laughed, shook his head, and went back into the kitchen to get a serving knife. The air was clear, and I decided to keep my mouth shut from then on.

That evening at ten-forty, my mother died. We were all beside her bed. We said the Memorare, and everyone placed a hand on Mom as we said the words to the prayer. I stood next to my dad and watched him as the words came out of my mouth. The tears in his eyes slowly rolled down his face, but he never stopped saying the prayer. He looked right at Mom and held her hand. The look of love and loss in his eyes was the saddest thing I had ever seen.

The next morning was cloudy and snowy. It was a wet snow, but it was sticking to the ground because it had been so cold. I walked into the kitchen to find Sister Pat sitting at the table, helping my dad choose readings and songs for the funeral. There were other people in the kitchen, but I just stood next to the chop block, not wanting to move. I wasn't talking or listening to anyone, and I had no reason to stay. But I couldn't physically move. Even if I could have, I wasn't sure where else to go. I wanted to be with everyone else; I didn't want to be alone.

The doorbell rang, and that was the motivation I needed. I opened the front door to find sweet Caroline. She was covered with snow, and her eyes were red from crying. She was talking fast because she was so upset. I cried instantly when I saw her. I had wanted her with me, but I didn't know how to tell her about my mother. She said that her mom had told her. Caroline asked her what she should do. Her mother replied, "Would you want Megan with you, if you were in her shoes?"

Caroline looked at me very seriously and said, "I put my boots on, grabbed the banana bread I had just made, and got here as fast as I could. I left in such a hurry my dad didn't even ask me if I had my list." It was the perfect thing to say, and we both burst out laughing through our tears.

After she left, I went back to the kitchen. Sister Pat was talking with Helen and Fiona at the table while Dad was on the phone. I just stood there again; this time waiting for something to happen. My mom had been in the kitchen my entire life. She was cooking one meal, preparing for the next, cleaning dishes, or reading the newspaper and drinking coffee. If I ever needed to ask her anything, I would always find her in the kitchen. Maybe she would be talking on the phone at the kitchen table or writing down her grocery list for the menu she had planned for the week. I guess it was the place in the house that I felt closest to Mom. I assumed my position by the chop block and just waited quietly. I didn't know what to do with myself.

"Thank you, I will get that over to you sometime today." Dad hung up the phone and told Sister Pat that he needed an outfit for Mom to be buried in. I asked him if I could pick the outfit out for him. I knew this was the perfect job for me, and I so desperately wanted to do something. Dad turned to me and smiled.

"You know what, Megan? I know your mom would rather you pick out her clothes than me. She always turned to you when she thought something was missing in one of her outfits, didn't she? Thank you, sweetie. I really appreciate it."

I ran upstairs to Mom's and Dad's closet. I went directly to her side, the left, and ran my hands over her clothes. I knew my job wasn't that important, but I finally felt like I could really do something, even if it was minute. Even as I ran my hands over Mom's clothes, pretending to deliberate, I knew exactly what outfit I would choose for her. It was her favorite.

First, I looked for her black velvet blazer. Then, I found her ivory ruffled blouse. Her full-length plaid skirt that had brown and black with hints of ivory was in the back of the closet. Mom always wore her brown boots with that outfit. But I had a dilemma. *Does she need anything on her feet?* I pictured her wearing her boots in heaven and singing to St. Peter, "These boots were made for walking…." That was the first time I had smiled in over a week. *It's perfect*, I thought to myself. *She's going to look beautiful.*

Once I pulled the outfit with her boots and laid it on the bed, I noticed a shoebox on Mom's side of the closet. I thought about it and knew it was wrong, but I took it off the shelf and looked inside. The box was full of letters that people had written to Mom during the last couple of months. I could tell from the postmarks. I sat down on the floor of the closet and started to read letter after letter.

I must have read fifteen letters from friends and relatives. What shocked me the most was that they all knew how sick she had been. They knew she was dying. I dropped the last letter to the floor, shocked and angry. No one told me Mom was going to die. *How could they have known this long and not told me?*

Helen walked in the room and asked if I needed help with Mom's clothes. She found me sitting on the floor, and she saw the box and letters scattered all around me. She realized what I was doing. "Megan, put those back! They weren't meant for you to read. Put them back where you found them! Dad is waiting for you downstairs!"

I stood up, folded them exactly the way I found them, and put them back in the box. I put the lid on, turned out the light, and closed the door behind me. I walked downstairs and handed Dad the clothes that I had picked out for Mom, emotionless. I went into the living room and fell into a chair like a brick falling from a roof. I heard the door close behind me, and the house fell silent. I stared at the Charlie Brown Christmas tree and thought, *how come I didn't know? Why didn't anybody tell me?*

My mind wanders back to my conversation with Mrs. Skowren in this very room only a few days earlier. *She did try to tell me. I heard the doctor, too. The cancer was everywhere. I'm so stupid. How could I have ever thought she would get better?* I was too selfish to even see that my own mother was dying. I began to cry, but it was too late.

We had two funerals for Mom. The first was held on Friday, December 27th, in Dayton, Ohio, just nine days after she came home from the hospital. The Catholic Church was standing room only. Jimmy Dunne and Caroline were there to show their support for me. I saw them from the window of the hearse. We never talked, but our eyes spoke to one another.

There was a poster-size picture of Mom at the funeral that was taken about six months before she died. It was from one of Fiona's swim meets. The picture captured everything about Mom and her love for life. She was smiling as she clapped her hands, and all you could see around her face was the beautiful blue sky. I remembered that Mom and Dad were sitting initially, but when Fiona started winning her race, Mom stood up to get a better view. My dad was captivated by her and took the picture while he was still sitting. They always say a picture is worth a thousand words, but this one said just one: *happiness*. Mom's hair had started growing back, she was watching her youngest daughter win the hundred-meter butterfly, and she thought she was beating her worst nightmare, cancer.

I overheard my dad tell Helen to tell Fiona that it was okay to cry at the funeral. But Fiona never showed any emotion at the viewing the night before or during the service. She was only twelve years old.

Dad hosted a luncheon after the funeral and most of our extended family members came to show their respects. We didn't have a burial service in Dayton since she was going to be buried in Dubuque, Iowa, beside her mom. People were everywhere, and it was overwhelming. I felt like an outsider watching someone else's life fall apart.

The next day, my dad packed us up, and we traveled the eight hours to Iowa for her burial. We stayed at my Grandpa Delany's house, and it was so quiet. Nine people in a seventeen hundred square foot house, and you could hear a pin drop at any given time. My grandfather paced in the dining room for most of the time we were there. He kept jingling his change in his pockets as he walked. I knew it was nervous energy. I couldn't understand why my mom was buried in Iowa when we lived in Ohio. Maybe it was a part of truly going home.

On Monday morning, we had the second funeral and burial service for Mom. It was December 30th in Dubuque, Iowa, where the average temperature was twenty-one degrees. Ironically, there was a cold front hitting the Midwest with a wind chill of ten below zero that day. I tried to keep warm in the car on the way to the cemetery by rubbing my hands together with mittens that didn't match. One was actually a sock, and the other one was a mitten I found under the seat of the car. My shoulders were almost touching my knees because the shiver running down my spine made it hard to sit up straight. We came to a stoplight, and I looked out the back window of our '76 Chevy station wagon. Enough cars to fill a parking lot followed us in one lane of the highway to the cemetery. The rolling hills of farmland on both sides of the road were covered with several inches of snow. The prosperous corn crops from the summer had died and lay beneath it. The only sign of life was the farmhouse that I saw in the distance. Smoke billowed from the chimney, and I could see a candle in each of the windows. It reminded me of a Norman Rockwell photograph. A beautiful Christmas wreath with a red bow hung on the front door, and tiny white lights covered the greenery that draped over the entryway. I wondered what kind of Christmas they were having. Surely, it was better than ours. *It's not supposed to be this way,* I thought. I wanted to wake up from this nightmare and have things back the way they were. I wanted my mom back and the life we all had, but I knew it would never be the same.

The service was nice, I guess. Actually, I couldn't understand why people said that. It was a funeral, and they are depressing. We were all thinking of our own mortality and how overwhelmed we were with pain because we would never talk to or see my mom again. Everyone's eyes were swollen from crying, and we didn't have enough tissues to go around. The lump in my throat was pushing the limit. But somehow, through all the condolences and countless hugs from relatives and friends of my mom's that I had never met before, I remembered what Father Anthony had told me. He was the Catholic priest that worked at the hospital. He apparently knew more about my own mother than I did because he once said to me, "Your mother's faith always gives her peace."

I knew that my mom's body had been at peace for about five days, but I selfishly wanted her with us. I knew she wasn't suffering any more. There would be no more surgeries, chemotherapy, or oxygen tanks because it was over. Or as a woman of faith would believe, it had just begun for her—eternity in heaven. Maybe that was what Father Anthony meant. She knew she was going to be in heaven a lot longer than any suffering she could possibly endure on earth. But peace wasn't something I was thinking or feeling. The thought that kept haunting me was that through a viewing, two funerals, and a burial service, I never said good-bye.

Chapter Seven

Rocks

"Welcome, folks, to Dayton, Ohio. The current temperature is a balmy seventy-four degrees," the flight attendant announced. I turned my phone on and found that I had six new voicemails.

- "Megan, this is Stacy Newton, and I wanted to know if Ginny could babysit tonight? I will try you at the house."
- "Mom, this is Ginny. Do we have to get dressed up for the luncheon? Liam is wearing an AC/DC t-shirt. What should I wear? Call me, please? Oh, and I need the number to the pizza place."
- "Megan, this is Meehan. I'm speechless. I don't know how you pulled off this unbelievable day. I just can't stop smiling. It was so great! I just left the bar with the girls, and we all were talking about how wonderful this party was. Call me please. I loved the posters! They were hysterical…. Wait, I only have thirty seconds. I loved every minute! I cried when the kids sang. It was sup…." The operator's recording interrupted Meehan's message, "To erase, press seven. To save in the archives, press nine."

I pressed nine.

- "Megan, it was great!!! Call me later!" (That was Amy.)
- "Moller, it's Mark, I did the Oprah bit, and it was good. Good call, but you still owe me cupcakes and cookies next year."
- "Megan, its Fiona…. Meet me at the baggage claim. Hurry!"

I texted her that I was walking to the baggage claim and that I would see her in five.

Her jeep pulled up to me like clockwork. The window on the passenger side rolled down and she said, "Hello, my friend."

"Hello!"

She opened the hatch, and I threw my suitcase in the back, closed it, and opened the passenger's door. The policeman signaled us to get out of the way.

"We are leaving right now," I say as I jump into the front seat. I turn to Fiona. "I'm so exhausted and glad to be here at the same time! Please tell me that we are going to sit at a bar and eat delicious food because I don't have the energy to do anything else."

"Well, I thought we could ride bikes to dinner tonight."

"What?"

"Yep, it's an easy ride, and we could pick up the rocks down by the river and have dinner at the Submarine House. They have the best cheese steak sandwich."

"The rocks...the ones you want to take to Mom's grave?" Fiona had called a few weeks prior to our trip. She wanted us to take something with us to Mom's grave that we could leave forever. Flowers would die, but she had found these cool rocks at the river near her house. They were naturally formed in the river and the minerals in the water made them have unique colors. Helen and I agreed that it would be a great idea to pick individual rocks for each one of us and leave them at Mom's grave. That way, she could always have a little piece of all of us.

"Yep, those! I thought we could pick out the rocks for the family and then have fun cooccckkkktails and a yummy delicious dinner, while getting a little exercise, as well."

"Ugh! Okay, fine, let's do it. But you are so buying the first round, deal?"

"Deal."

We arrived at Fiona's house, and her husband Sterling called on the phone. Fiona talked to him for about ten minutes, and I decided to change clothes for our bike ride while I waited for them to hang up. I found a pair of jeans from The Collection and grabbed a sweater. Just three hours before, I was sweating my bum off in the subtropics and now I needed a sweater. By the time I got situated, Fiona was already in the driveway with the bikes.

"Nice bikes. When did you guys get these?" I asked as I inspected the tires and basket on the bike.

"Sterling got them from his mom, and we have been riding them everywhere. We started riding the bike trail a couple of months ago, and now we ride three days a week just to get some exercise. We love it."

"Cool, which one is for me?"

"You get the one with the basket, and I'll ride his."

"Wow, I get the basket. Cool beans," I say.

"Yep, but that means you have to carry the rocks back."

"Wait? You make it sound like they're going to be heavy."

Fiona started laughing and peddled fast, so I couldn't try to trade bikes with her. We biked out of her neighborhood and down North Fairfield Road for about three blocks downhill. Then, as we were stopped at a traffic light, I noticed the funeral home in the background. Mom had been there twenty-five years earlier. Fiona didn't say anything about the funeral home, which I thought was strange, but I didn't say anything either. I couldn't imagine how I would feel if I had to pass by it every day to and from work. *Would it be a constant reminder of what could have been or what was?*

The light turned green, and we peddled on Dayton's Xenia Road. This easy bike ride was getting a little harder. We weren't going downhill anymore, and considering I'm a physical wreck, I was beginning to struggle.

"We're here. The trail is right over there," Fiona yelled back since she was ahead of me. The path opened up like a two-lane road just for bikes. I'm not sure when the change happened, but we went from a busy city to complete serenity. Huge weeping willow trees were gently blowing on each side of the path cascading downward. They almost touched the road and looked like they were waving hello to us. There were bikers and runners all along the path. The temperature was perfect, the breeze was calm, and the scenery was beautiful. I actually forgot I was tired because the beauty distracted me.

"Why have I never seen this before?" I asked Fiona

"I know! Sterling and I found this a couple of months ago when we rode to get margaritas at this cute Mexican place. The only problem with doing that is we have to be sure not to drink too many before we have to ride back home. Oh, and we have to get home before dark because there aren't any lights on this trail."

"Perfect," I laughed, "What time is it?"

"Late…we have to hustle. Okay, here it is. Put your bike against the tree and follow me."

We walked for about a quarter of a mile on this worn path covered with leaves. Fiona led the way. She pushed branches back so that she could pass, but then they kept springing back and hitting me in the head. The crackling of leaves beneath our feet and birds chirping were the only sounds. The silence was so peaceful and foreign to me since I live in a three-ring circus twenty-four/seven. It didn't feel like any place I had ever been. I felt so far away from my life. Then my phone rang, and it brought me back.

"Hello?" I couldn't hear anyone on the other end. "Hello?"

"Who is it, Megan?" Fiona asked.

"I lost the call. Apparently we are in nowhere land because I don't have any reception. How much longer 'til we're there?"

At that instant, we looked down at the Little Miami River. "This is so pretty! Why haven't I ever seen this river before? Fiona, those are rapids. They're not huge, but they're rapids. Wow, this is so pretty. I feel like we are in Colorado or something!" I yell at the top of my lungs, "BOOOOBBBBBBY! CIIIIIIIINDY!!!!! Oh Mike, where are they?"

"That never gets old for you, does it?" Fiona says in a disgusted voice.

"Nope! That was my favorite episode of the Brady Bunch. Remember how Bobby and Cindy got lost in the Grand Canyon?"

"Right, right, right," Fiona mumbles.

"Hey, how come we never came down here before?"

"We did," Fiona replies. She is annoyed that I don't believe her. "We went kayaking down this river probably ten times."

"You know what? I believe there was a lot of drinking on those boat rides. Maybe that's why I don't remember." We both chuckle. "Speaking of drinking, let's take care of business, so we can have a cocktaillllllll."

"Okay, we need eight rocks: six for us kids, one for Dad, and one for Uncle John."

"I think this is such a good idea, Fiona, to leave these rocks at Mom's grave. You're right, it's like we are leaving a little piece of us with her."

"I know, I may be the youngest, but I am definitely the wisest."

"I know, I know. Hey, how about this salt-and-pepper looking one for Dad?"

"That's good."

I walked over to the water and found so many beautiful rocks, all different shapes and colors. The sound of the rushing water was soothing as I continued to search for the perfect rocks that represented our family. I pulled one from the pile, "Oh, my stars, this one looks like a gold bar. Let's get this one for Jack because he has so much money."

"Is that even a real rock? I have never seen anything like that before! It looks like a dollar bill."

"That's why it's perfect for Jack."

"What should we get for Helen?"

"This big blue rock," I say as I hold it up for Fiona to see.

"Why big and blue?"

"Because she is a big part of our lives, and she became our other mom. Personally, I like it because it will mess with her head since it is big. She's automatically going to think it has something to do with her weight. What do you think?"

"I like it. She is a big part of our lives, and I like the fact that it's blue. It looks calm and soothing, and she has always been there for us. You're right, she is gonna think it has something to do with her weight. This one is definitely Helen's."

"I'm putting it in the basket! Okay, three down and five to go. Keep looking because time is of the essence."

We both walked along the bank, and the only sounds we heard were the rushing water from the river and the leaves in the trees blowing in the wind. Fiona and I continued to pick up rocks and rationalize how they represented each family member's traits or characteristics. We looked at them and then put them back down as we searched for the perfect ones.

My mind starts to wander as I think about the rocks in my life. My family and friends have been there to help me through the rough times. They, my rocks, have always been by my side when I have needed them the most, whether I needed a good listener or a shoulder to cry on. I can call Helen and Fiona at any given time of the day and know they have my back. They support me, listen to me, and always encourage me to keep my head up. I love when Fiona tells me to hold on when I call her because she then calls Helen, and the three of us have a conference call to talk about whatever problem we have at the time. A friend once told me, "all we need is one rock in our lives to get us through the rough times." It's true. You just need one. But I'm lucky. I have a quarry.

"Hey, wait, I found the perfect rock! It's so delicate and beautiful when it hits the light. You have to see this one, Fiona! It really is pretty. It reminds me of…." I can't even say it without laughing. "Me."

"Really? Now *I* need a drink. Ew, I just stepped on something. Oh shit, no! Really, is that mud or dog crap on my shoe?"

"I can't smell anything, so I think its mud."

We both laugh.

"Okay, we really do need to kick it up a notch because we have to be home before dark, and I'm worried this is taking too long." Fiona scanned the rocks around her.

"I feel like we are ten years old again. We have to be home before dark."

"Hello? Your maturity level hasn't changed since you were ten."

"That's why I'm a perfect kindergarten teacher. Hey, Fiona,

what about this rock over here for Murphy? You know, considering he and Helen are the Irish twins, why don't we get them the same rock?"

"Wait, it's the same color, but it's smaller."

"She is definitely going to think it has to do with her weight. I love it."

"Who else do we need to find rocks for?"

"Shamus, Uncle John, and I still need rocks," Fiona answered as she walked away from me with her head down, not wanting to miss anything good.

"This one looks like Mom's birthstone. Isn't it pretty? I think this one should be yours because of its color and since you were Mom's favorite."

Before I finish my sentence, Fiona has put the stone in the basket.

"I like this one for Uncle John. It's solid and true, just like him."

"Okay, now Shamus needs one, and they all are starting to look alike to me. Hold on, Fiona, look at this one. The one side is rough and the other side is completely smooth. Does that make you think of anyone?"

"Yes, it's perfect for the transformation he has made in his life."

"I love that we are *done*. Let's have that delicious cheese steak sandwich and some cocktailllllls."

"Okay, let's roll."

The bike ride to the restaurant was a little tough because it was uphill, and I was trying to keep up with Fiona. I forgot what it's like to not have any kids and to have time to work out. Fiona works out on a regular basis and is in fantastic shape. I, on the other hand, don't even have time to have regular bowel movements. Plus, the added weight of the rocks definitely made it a lot more challenging. Fiona kept making fun of me because I said hello to everybody that passed us on the trail. All of my "hey, hi, how you doing?" left me breathless.

Fiona laughed, saying I was going to cause an accident because I was catching people off guard, and they were losing their rhythms. I told her to shut up and that's just what we do in the South. She looked at me and said, "Flossy, you're in *Ohio*, not the South."

Within ten minutes, we were walking our bikes up the hill to the restaurant. We chose to sit on the patio, so we could keep our eyes on the bikes and our precious stones. The drinks were delicious, and the food was even better. I was with my little sister talking about old boyfriends and married life, laughing hysterically.

When I look at Fiona, I see success, confidence, and wisdom beyond her thirty-eight years. She's lived in England and has traveled throughout Europe. I think of Fiona like a fine wine because she gets better with age. She probably has taught me more about myself and about being the person I'm meant to be than anyone else in my life. Maybe it's her artsy side that keeps peeling away the layers in my life and helps me focus on what's important and what's not. Sometimes I think she's the grown-up version of how I want to be with my husband when the kids move out someday. She and Sterling take long vacations, play golf at the club, and go to dinner without using coupons. As my dad would say, "they're living the dream." She has a saying that I love, and I use it all the time because it encompasses a true meaning about people. If she likes them she'll say, "They got salt!" The expression doesn't even need an explanation.

Chapter Eight

Tough Actin'

The ride home was a lot easier. It might have been the margaritas, or the fact that it was downhill some of the way. Whatever the case, I was enjoying it immensely. Fiona always makes everything fun. She has this childlike quality about her that makes you want to be excited about whatever you're doing with her. Every time we get together, my stomach gets a better workout from laughter than it ever would with a trainer at the gym. When we start laughing, it's the "I can't breathe I'm laughing so hard" kind of laughter that doesn't happen enough in everyday life. You have to take it when you can get it. It's the best drug I know of, and I'm a heavy user.

One of the things that I remember about my mom is her laughter: It was addictive. She knew how to have fun and could light up any room with her smile and sense of humor. Fiona got it from her.

We were two blocks from Fiona's house when she said, "We need to stop by the store."

"Sure," I say since she is now riding the bike with all the rocks and weight.

However, we actually ride our bikes through the Beer Drive Thru. The Beer Drive Thru is a drive-thru for people who want to buy beer, wine, cigarettes, or snacks without leaving their cars. It's such a cool concept. I wish we had these back in South Carolina.

Fiona pulls her bike right next to mine as if we are in a car. She is the driver, and I am on the passenger side. I can't stop laughing.

"Hi, Fiona," says the gal working.

Fiona leans over to me and whispers in my ear. "I'm very popular."

"Or the town drunk," I whisper back.

"Right, right, right," she says sarcastically, and we both almost fall off our bikes.

"Fiona, what can I get for you?" says the gal.

"Can we have a bottle of chardonnay, a six-pack of Guinness, a bag of Doritos, and a pack of Ultra Lights?"

The gal working the store was running around trying to get our order ready for us. She was probably wondering how we were going to carry everything since our basket was already filled with rocks.

"Are you *serious*? I thought you quit smoking, Fiona!"

"I have definitely cut back! I swear I'm working on quitting for good."

"Seriously? Fiona, Mom died of *lung cancer*. Why are you still smoking?" I know I'm being a hypocrite, but she's my baby sister. I'm supposed to stop her from making the same mistakes I've made.

"Eventually, I will quit. Just not this weekend. We've got way too much to deal with, and I'm going to need a smoke."

"$26.75 is your total."

I reached in my pocket for some cash. "I got this," says Fiona.

"Thanks for your business and be careful on those bikes!"

We left the beer-thru with me carrying the six-pack of Guinness and the Doritos and Fiona carrying the wine and smokes. We laughed and talked all the way home. We made it there just before dark. "Perfect timing," I told her. We parked the bikes in the garage and carried our supplies inside the house.

"Do you want beer or wine?" Fiona asked.

"I want a beer."

"Got it. Let's sit outside, so I can smoke. Can you light the candles out on the table? I will be out in a sec."

I walked outside to the table on their patio, found a spray bottle, and started spraying. Then I lit a couple of candles and patiently waited for my beer. I had to say, it was so nice to be waited on. Having three kids and a husband, I am always on the go. I'm a short order cook, nurse, and maid on a good day. So when I'm waiting on someone who is doing something for me, its foreign territory, but I am eager to accept the challenge.

Fiona came outside holding a beer and wine in one hand and the bag of Doritos in the other. "I know we just ate, but I can always find room for a couple of chips," she said as wine swayed from side to side in her glass.

"Perfect. Thanks for the beer. How about put the bag in the middle of the table, so I can reach them, too."

"The stereo is on. What would you like to hear?"

"Considering you don't have Karen Carpenter, I will let you decide."

"Seriously, your music repertoire sucks. I have really good music that you will like. Just sit back, enjoy, and for the love of God, try and learn something."

The breeze was nice enough to keep the bugs away, and I put my sweater on to ward off the chill of the night. I put my feet on her table and leaned back in my chair. "It's so good to be home."

"I'm glad you're here," Fiona said as she raised her glass to my beer.

"Hey, have you played golf with Dad lately?" I ask as I take a sip of my beer and reach for the bag of Doritos.

"Sterling and I played with him last week out at the Country Club of the North. We always have so much fun with him. He's totally in his element when he's golfing, and I love that I can take him there. He loves that it's free. He and Sterling actually played pretty well, too. I, on the other hand, played horrifically," she replied as she lit her cigarette and dropped the lighter on the table.

"Does he still bring his peanuts in his golf bag?" I ask, repositioning my feet.

"Of course he does, and every time we are on the turn getting ready to play the back nine, I always ask him if he wants a hot dog or a soda."

"What does he say?

"'No, Squirt, I'm fine.' I override his answer and get him one of each anyway, and you should see his eyes light up when I hand them to him. It's hilarious. It's like he's a little kid."

"You know what? I think Liam got his alligator arms from his grandpa. Why doesn't he want to spend any money? He is such a piece of work. But it's even funnier he still calls you 'Squirt.'"

"Oh, let me tell you this. Usually when we play, he and I are on a team together, and we share a golf cart. So when he's looking for his ball on the fairway, I have to drop him off and drive around to find my ball, which is usually on the opposite side. Anyway, before I leave I say, 'Dad, do you need anything before I go?' You know, like another club or something from his golf bag. When he answers the question, Megan, I swear he is talking about more than just his golf clubs."

"What does he say?"

"'Squirt, I've got everything I need.' He always has this half grin on his face, and I can't help but smile. I never get tired of hearing him say that to me. Isn't that cute?" She takes a hit of her cigarette and exhales the smoke, "He says it every time."

I nod and say, "Hey, did you call Helen today?"

"I did. She asked what time we were leaving in the morning, just making sure we were going to be on time."

"You're such a liar. *She* called *you* because she didn't know what time her flight was leaving, didn't she?" I asked.

"I sent her the itinerary, and she's good to go with the name of the airline."

Instantly, I picture Helen. She definitely needs a break. She is a full-time first grade teacher, spends about three hours driving her car every day between work, taking her four kids to school, and picking them up from sporting events. She's the type of person who thinks of everyone but herself. A good day to Helen would be roller-blading in her neighborhood and ending the evening with a glass of wine. It doesn't take much to make her happy. Of all of us, she reminds me the most of my mom because she raises her kids how we were raised. She's determined, never gives up, and gives everything she has to her family, asking for nothing in return. She and her husband, Tim, have encouraged their kids with sports and musical instruments, and most importantly, with faith. Mom would be so proud of her. Their house may not be an Ethan Allen showroom, and the laundry may never be caught up, and it may take a while for things to get fixed after they break. But I think Helen's philosophy is that it's more important to give her kids what she had growing up: a home that is full of love, the encouragement to believe that anything is possible, and a sense of humor. She is constantly teaching those around her about life through her unconditional love. I will always admire her selfless attitude.

"When I think of Helen, I think of the last time I was at their house in West Palm. The kids and I took a train down to visit her. She and Tim were great about having seven kids in one house for a couple of days. One day I followed Helen from the kitchen table outside to the driveway. Tim was sitting at the end of it, wearing his Pittsburgh Steelers jersey and shorts and drinking a beer on this gorgeous Saturday afternoon. He yelled, 'Babe, get out of the way. The boys are having a basketball tournament, and I'm the referee.' Helen tripped over a beach bag that had been lying in the same spot for four days. It was still holding the towels and sunscreen. The boys stopped the game and looked at her. 'Colleen was supposed to put that away,' one of them yelled.

"'I'll pick it up,' Helen responded. Gymnastics mats covered the floor of the garage, and five neighborhood girls including Colleen and Maggie were practicing their back pike landings in the yard. The trash was overflowing because we had ordered about eight pizzas the night before, and it was hard to tell what was recycling and what was trash because it all flowed together. Every kid in the neighborhood popped in at least once a day while we were there. Their house was such a fun place to be. Huge Tupperware containers holding bats, baseballs and basketballs, some flat and some full of air, lined the walls of the garage. Stray wrappers, Popsicle sticks, banana peels, and empty water bottles somehow found their way into these boxes, too.

"They had doors from inside the house stacked in a corner of their garage, and the kids used them as props during their annual Survivor Tournament. Three or four boogie boards and beach chairs were all thrown together with seaweed and sand stuck to the bottoms. I looked up and noticed Tim walking towards me, throwing an empty beer can into a container like it was a basketball. Helen was looking at me and had her back to him. He tapped her on the ass as he passed, overwhelmed with his own talent. 'I'd like to tap that, babe,' he teased. 'What's it like to be married to such a *man*, a *Pittsburgh man*? You know how much I love you? Hey, by the way, the Steelers are playing on Sunday, and the boys are going with me to the game.'

"He continued to talk as he walked to the outdoor refrigerator. He moved the water balloons to the side as he pulled out a Miller Lite beer. He opened it, took a sip, and asked, 'You think you could clean the garage?'

"Helen just looked at him like he was crazy. All of a sudden Tim dodged a basketball that was catapulting towards him in one swift movement. He walked to the end of the driveway and assumed his position on his sand-filled, seaweed-plagued chair at the end of the driveway. Helen looked at me, laughed, and said, 'Yeah, I'll get right on that after I landscape the yard and lay the hardwood floors.'"

"I love how she makes the kids sort socks when they get in trouble. That sock basket must hold two hundred mismatched socks. Remember the neighborhood dog, Sunny, that used to open her front door every day and just walk into her house?" Fiona adds.

I nod. "I know we give Tim a hard time, but I love him. If we called him right now and asked for money or a place to stay, he wouldn't even hesitate. He's a textbook Pittsburghian."

"I know, me too. He always makes me laugh. He's so crazy."

"Actually, I think he started the Suson Fuson thing, didn't he?" I asked her.

"Poor Suson, I didn't even know her real name was Suzanne until she introduced herself to someone while we were on one of our trips one year."

"What time is it?"

"Twelve-thirty. Why?" Fiona replied.

"Do you think she's packed yet?"

"Who, you mean Suson?"

"No, Helen! I bet she's sitting on the porch with Tim, and they're drinking some wine, and she hasn't even packed yet."

"You're probably right." We both laugh at Helen because we know her too well.

"I can't wait to see her."

"Me either!" Fiona adds.

"I look forward to these trips every year. Hey, what is that smell? I think the bug spray is working because nothing has bitten me, but the smell is strange."

"Wait, what bug spray?" Fiona questions.

I pick up the spray and pass it to Fiona.

She puts the light from her cigarette close to the bottle and reads the can.

"Oh, my gosh! I have been looking for this for the past two days. It needs to go in my suitcase!"

"What the hell is it?"

"It's my Tough Actin' Tinactin. Sterling and I have a raging outbreak of athlete's foot, and this stuff is the only thing that works."

I laugh so hard my sides hurt, and I can't breathe. "Are you serious? What the heck is it doing on your patio table?"

"Sterling must have brought it out here to use it. Megan, you have no idea how bad your feet itch when you have athlete's foot. You're miserable, and this is the only stuff that works. When I spray it on my feet, they burn so bad that I want to scream at the top of my lungs, but it works. 'Make it hurt so good,' my friend." She raised her wine glass to me to toast, "To Tough Actin' Tinactin, cheers!"

"Cheers," I say back and laugh, but all I can think is, *thank goodness I brought my flip-flops for the shower.*

Chapter Nine

Both Sides

B *eeeeeeeeep!*
My phone alarm burst into my dreams, and I frantically reached for it under my pillow to shut it off. Finding it in the dark wasn't easy. Fiona had me sleeping in her guest room, which consisted of four blankets stretched out on the floor. No bed, but after all the cocktails we drank, I could have slept on a woodpile and wouldn't have complained. I wiped the sleep from my eyes and reached for the door. The light was on in the kitchen, and Fiona was brewing coffee for the car ride. She looked at me and piped up, "How did you sleep?"

All I could muster out was, "I think…good?"

"You think?"

"Well, we just went to bed like three hours ago."

"Good, I thought you would be tired."

We both laughed because it was ridiculously early, and I think I was still drunk.

"We have a long day ahead of us. Do what you gotta do. We are leaving in fifteen!" Fiona advised.

Twelve minutes later, at four-forty, we were backing out of Fiona's driveway and heading to Chicago. We were officially on our way to pick up Helen and thus, one step closer to Mom's grave. We were quiet at first—tired from our long night. After an hour or so, though, we couldn't stop talking. I guess that's just what we do. We try and cram as much as we can into the days we spend together. Once the coffee kicked in, we were talking about everything under the sun.

Fiona has always been a music buff. I think it really started when she and her husband were dating, and they followed the Grateful Dead one summer. They followed the band on the "Further Tour" for twelve days all through the mid-west. They saw ten different shows and maybe showered three times during those hot days of summer. She knows her music, most artists, and usually all of the lyrics to any song on the radio. "There's always a story, and when you know the story, the song means more," Fiona told me.

As the miles rolled under us, she educated me on Bob Dylan, Eric Clapton, and Joni Mitchell. Out of everyone, I liked Joni Mitchell the most. I think we were about ninety miles outside of Indianapolis, and Fiona played one of her songs called "Both Sides Now" that she had re-recorded a couple of years before. Apparently, the song had more meaning to her as she lived life. She viewed things differently than she did when she first recorded it. *Don't we all feel that way in some sense?* I thought to myself.

The symphony of violins in the background was hauntingly beautiful. Listening to the song, I sat mesmerized staring out of my window as huge windmills appeared on both sides of the highway. Fiona explained to me that it was the Fowler Ridge Wind Farm, which consists of over five hundred turbine windmills. They were probably seventy-five to one hundred feet high. These windmills surrounded us on both sides of Highway 52. They were all lined in perfect formation, and if you looked closely, you could see them moving.

My mind was racing as I listened to the words of the song "Both Sides Now," watching these massive windmills move. The clouds came out like a coverlet casing the sky, and the rain started to gently hit the windshield. To me, it felt like a slap of reality. I came to understand what we were really doing. We were going to our mother's grave. We hadn't been there in fourteen years.

It was a profound moment for me. The windshield wipers whisked back and forth as the rain came down harder and harder, and it reminded me of the story of Don Quixote, of all things. I can't say I remember a lot of my required reading as a kid, but Don Quixote was unique. He stuck with me because he was so out there. He was a middle-aged man on a journey to defend the helpless and destroy the wicked. As I looked out the window, my reflection stared back at me, and I could vividly see the crow's feet around my eyes, reminding me that I'm middle-aged. I then thought about Don Quixote's sidekick, Sancho, who wasn't the sharpest tool in the shed. I immediately turned to look at my driver, Fiona.

She noticed me staring at her and asked, "What? Why are you looking at me?" I couldn't help but laugh out loud.

I turned my head back to look at the windmills. I started to question myself about my possible likeness to Don Quixote. I was fighting feelings and personal demons that I didn't have a chance at beating. *Had I actually thought about how hard it would be on all of us to see Mom's grave? What were we all trying to accomplish on the journey we were on? Did I expect that visiting her grave was going to give me closure? Would it give me peace?* I started to have my doubts about everything. The song continued to play in the background.

But now they only block the sun
They rain and snow on everyone
So many things I would have done
But clouds got in my way
I've looked at clouds from both sides now

From up and down, and still somehow
It's cloud illusions I recall
I really don't know clouds at all

Maybe this was a sign just for me. I couldn't look away from the windmills. I felt a lump in my throat and tears well in my eyes. The green lush countryside was so peaceful as these massive objects moved gently, as if directing us onward. The rain came down faster and heavier on the car. *Keep the faith,* I thought, *just keep the faith. This is the right thing to do.*

The words to "Both Sides Now" are so ironic and fitting to my life. I realized, *"I really don't know life at all."*

This was the second time in less than twenty-four hours that something took me totally by surprise. I was amazed at how something could change so quickly, and I didn't even realize it was happening. First the bike path and now these windmills...I wondered what else was going to take me by surprise.

Chapter Ten

Tampons, Underwear, and Burt's Bees Lip Balm

We arrived at O'Hare International Airport about twenty-five minutes after Helen's flight landed. We drove aimlessly around outside the baggage claim.

"Where are we meeting Helen?" I asked Fiona.

"I told her to be outside by the arrivals near the American Airlines baggage claim."

That didn't seem so bad, until we arrived on the lower level of the baggage claim and found approximately a thousand people waiting for buses, taxis, and rides. Cars were lined up blocking traffic, taxis were beeping their horns looking for perspective clients, and I was yelling out the front window: "Helen?"

All while Fiona was driving her car ten miles per hour.

"How are we going to find her? This is ridiculous. Why doesn't she have a phone?" I asked.

"Mike had a cross-country meet today, and he needed Helen's, remember? *You* told *me*." Fiona replied as she tried to maneuver around the taxi cabs waiting for patrons.

"Do we even know what she's wearing?"

"No, but I do know that she is carrying a backpack that is probably packed with lip balm and tampons."

We both laugh out loud. "Do you think she remembered to pack underwear this time? I told her she better because she isn't wearing mine."

Before Fiona could answer, I shouted, "Fiona, drive slower! Helen! Helen! Hey, is that her? Pull up over here." Realizing it wasn't Helen after all, I turned back to Fiona. "Never mind, keep driving."

We drove around the airport again for the fourth time. I was growing impatient. "This is ridiculous! We are never going to find her."

Fiona's phone starts ringing, but it's a number she doesn't recognize. She lets it go to voicemail. After another lap around the airport, she decides to check the message. It's Helen.

"Hey, guys! I'm using this nice lady's phone from the flight, and I was just wondering where you guys are? You can call me back, but only if it's in the next couple minutes because her ride is here. Uhhm…okay check ya later…bye."

Fiona tries to call back, but doesn't get an answer. So we are back to looking at thousands of people and finding no Helen. *Good thing she's family*, I think to myself. *Otherwise, we would have dropped this one from our trips years ago.*

"Okay, go slow and look over there. Is that her over there? Helen?"

"No, that's not her, but there she is. Helen! I know it's her because she's putting lip balm on her lips." Fiona points her out of the crowd.

Helen sees us and waves her hands in the air. "Hey, guys!"

We pull up to the curb, and she scrambles into the back seat, a highlighter pink Hello Kitty backpack in tow. "Hello, my friends. I am so happy to see you," she squeals. "I have to call Tim and let him know I'm here."

"Here, you can use my phone," I say as I pass it to her in the back seat.

"How was your flight?" Fiona glances over her shoulder at Helen.

"I guess okay. I just slept the whole way. Tim and I sat out on the back porch last night, and I drank too much wine. Can you believe that? *And* I'm on my period, and it's ridiculous! I didn't pack much, so I hope you brought me some cute outfits, Megan.

And for the love of God, please tell me no white pants!" We all laugh at her exuberance.

"What did you pack, Helen?" I ask.

Helen fumbles around in her interesting choice of luggage to give us an accurate account. "I've got tampons, underwear, and Burt's Bees lip balm." Fiona and I laugh hysterically as Helen pulls the lip balm out of her bag and reapplies yet again. "You guys are idiots!" Helen rolls her eyes. "I packed some really cute outfits that Tim bought for me. I will even add them to The Collection if you're nice. So quit making fun of me. Did you guys get the rocks?"

She put the lid on her balm and placed it back in the backpack.

Fiona and I share a look so as not to give away hints at Helen's rock.

"Yep, the rocks are very cool. We spent a lot of time picking them out," I replied.

"I wish I could have been with you two. Did you guys have fun?"

"Need you ask?" Fiona looks at Helen in rear view mirror.

I turn around from the front seat, so I can look at Helen when I talk to her. "Helen, Fiona is very friendly with the beer-thru lady. Actually, I think she was disappointed when she saw me with her," I joke.

"Why does that always happen to you, Fiona?" Helen asks as she moves to the middle of the back seat to get a better view.

"I'm loved by all, my friends."

Helen pipes up from her new perch, "Okay, what's the plan? Are we going to stop by 1722 Van Buren Street?" She asks excitedly, hoping we will all agree to go to visit our childhood home. We were all born in Chicago, and we lived there through my early elementary school days. We moved to North Carolina briefly and later settled in Dayton when I was nine.

"I'm all for it, but when does Suson Fuson get in? Do you think we will have enough time?" Fiona asked.

"Her flight comes in around twelve-thirty, so we have two hours to kill. I printed directions, and we're fourteen miles from our old house. I say we go?"

"Okay, sounds good to me," Fiona replied.

"Fiona, when we come out of the airport, take I-190 East, then I-294 North. We all need to watch because it's only a couple of miles that we're on each highway."

We ride in silence for a few moments, each keeping our eyes peeled for a sign. I soon see it. "There it is! Turn here, Fiona," I say pointing, to the right. "Oh my goodness, I totally remember that building with the mirrored windows over there. I remember looking at that office building on our way home from Dubuque after visiting Grandpa Delany and knowing we were home."

"Okay, Fiona, take West Touchy, but it says here we are going to go east and then it looks like we need to take the first right on South River Road? It looks familiar, but if we didn't have a map, I don't think I could get to the house," Helen continued to look out the window, not wanting to miss anything.

"Hey, there's Van Buren up there to the left," I chime in excitedly.

"Oh, my gosh! This is so weird. I haven't been here in thirty years. That house looks exactly the same. Who used to live there? Does anybody remember their names?" I ask, feeling as though I'm re-telling a dream that I vaguely remember.

"I can't remember their names, but they took us to go see Bozo the Clown with them," Helen responded.

"Yeah, I remember that, Helen. They had two girls, right?" I ask.

"Yep. Here it is…1722 Van Buren."

We stare out of the windshield at our first home. Two men are standing on the front porch. One is wearing a tool belt, and they appear to be sizing up the front door.

"Wow, it looks so small and broken down. It looks like those guys are maybe trying to restore or repair the front entryway," Fiona observes.

"Remember how well-kept it used to be? Dad always had the yard so pretty, and Mom had the flower pots on the front porch filled with red geraniums. Look, the shutters are falling off over there," Helen replies.

"I wish we could go inside and look around," I say to my sisters.

But even as the words leave my lips, I think to myself, *I feel how this house looks, broken inside and in need of serious repair.*

Chapter Eleven

House Full of Memories

"Come on, I got this," Fiona demands. "We are going inside. Just follow me." She parks the car on the side of the road, right in front of 1722. We get out and start walking towards the house.

I can see one man smiling as we approach him. He has about four teeth missing and puts out his cigarette with his boot. The only thing I can tell about the other one is that he looks like a plumber, and he's bending over to pick up a hammer.

"Hello, ladies," Gentleman Number One greets us.

"Hey, it looks like you guys have your work cut out for you. A lot of things need to be done to this house. Who lives here?" Fiona questions as she continues to check out the house and waits for a response.

"My brother. He wants to put it up for sale. We got a couple things to do before he can put it on the market."

"We used to live here back in the '70s, and we were wondering if we could walk through the house for old time's sake," Helen asked.

"Well, nobody's inside, and he ain't got nothin' to steal. You pretty ladies look harmless enough."

He motioned for us to follow him, and we stepped over the tools and ladder that were lying on the pathway. When I made it to the front door stoop, I paused, imagining my mom and me sitting there every afternoon waiting for my brothers and sister to come home from school. I looked down the street and remembered the view vividly. I could still see the neighbor's flag flapping in the wind, letting the neighborhood kids know their pool was open. All summer, kids would run down the street with a towel in one hand and goggles in the other, hoping to be the first in the water.

The man opened the front door to the house, and more memories flooded my mind. To my left, I envisioned the old dining room table with eight chairs that served countless dinners. I heard snippets of family conversations about the day's events. I could see my parent's black leather chair with the matching ottoman in the corner of the living room. I pictured the green sofa where I perched to watch Sesame Street every morning at eleven. I visualized the pictures on the mantle of Grandpa Delany and my parents on their wedding day. I saw a statue of the Blessed Virgin and a decorative plate in a stand.

I turned to my right and walked over to the window where we used to set up the Christmas tree every year. I looked down at the Capel rug sprawled across the entire room over the hardwood floors. I recalled the countless times I was on my knees in this room saying the rosary with my family and practicing the Irish jig with my sisters for the shows we performed for everyone.

I cross the room to the stairwell, overwhelmed with emotions and memories of my childhood. I can see myself saying "good night" to my parents, the way I did every night, and running up those stairs to the bedroom that I shared with Helen and Fiona. I leaned toward the window halfway up the stairway. It overlooked the backyard, and I remembered the fort my dad built for us. Fort Buren was built on stilts about twelve feet high and also served as a home for the basketball hoop.

We all thought that it was the coolest fort ever. Mom even put old shower curtains in the windows so the rain and snow wouldn't get inside. They were green in color and gave the fort a homey feel. I wondered how many years it lasted after we left before the new owners tore it down. In the background, I heard Helen and Fiona talking to the brother of the owner, pulling me out of my reverie. They were asking questions about the previous owners and the neighbors.

"When your brother moved in here, was there a shuffle board court in the backyard?" Helen asked.

I continue to climb the stairs and am surprised by how much smaller everything is compared to my memory. The girls are now behind me, and we point out our old room.

"The boys had the corner room, and that one over there was Mom's and Dad's. They got the room with the closet. The boys' room was the biggest, right? Does anybody know for sure? I mean, they all look small if you ask me." I'm having a harder time remembering these details.

"No one was asking," Fiona replies with a straight face, but she can only hold it for a second before bursting into laughter.

"Idiot," I respond and roll my eyes. When I step into our old room, I am surprised that it is the size of a large pantry. "How in the Mary Jo did we get bunk beds and a crib in this room?"

"How did we have only one bathroom for eight people?" Helen asks.

"I can actually remember being potty trained in that bathroom."

"Um, that's because you were eight years old, Megan."

"I wasn't eight. I was maybe three and had a very active bladder."

"Right, right, right," Helen teases. I elbow her, and we chuckle. The man working on the house obviously enjoys our banter, too.

"Phil, I need you to come down here!" We hear the plumber guy yell over the laughter.

"Sorry, ladies, I gotta get back to work." We follow him downstairs and ask more questions about the neighbors. We inquired about one neighbor in particular: Mrs. Henschke.

"Yes, she still lives next door. Matter of fact, we saw her this morning."

"We have to walk over and say hello," I say to the girls as we reach the main level of the house.

"How much time do we have before Suson Fuson's flight arrives?" Helen asks. Of course, she wouldn't remember. She couldn't even remember when her own flight was coming into O'Hare, let alone Suson's.

Fiona looks at her watch. "Maybe an hour and a half, but we need to make it quick."

We walk across the driveway towards Mrs. Henschke's house, and the front door opens as we approach. She steps out onto her porch. Eighteen years had passed since we had last seen Mrs. Henschke, and I didn't know if she would remember us.

"Mrs. Henschke? Mrs. Henschke?" I call out.

Fiona cuts me off, "Mrs. Henschke, it's me, Fiona."

She looks at Fiona, her mouth wide open, and starts to tear up. "Helen, is that you and Meg? Oh girls, I can't believe it's you! Please come inside and have some coffee."

We all hugged, walked into her house, and settled on her sofa that overlooked Van Buren Street. Her house was just as I remembered it. We ran to Mrs. Henschke's when we got in trouble and needed to be consoled. This was where we came when we needed a sugar fix. Mr. Henschke, who we knew had passed away a couple of years before, would always supply us with licorice—endless supplies of the black stuff.

When I was five years old, Mr. Henschke taught me to ride a bike. He spent countless hours with me, encouraging me and running along beside me, telling me I could do it. "Keep peddling, Meggy Meg, I know you can do it!" He taught the boys to shoot guns. I'm not sure if my mom knew that, but Dad did. We always received unconditional love and support at the Henschke house. Every child should have a house and people like the Henschkes in their lives.

Mrs. Henschke told us about Bill, "The Womanizer," aka the mailman who delivered more than just the mail. She told us how Bill would leave his mail cart outside Mrs. Spieman's house for a couple of hours every Tuesday. She had personally endured some ridicule when she invited Bill into her house for coffee one day. Mrs. H explained that she was simply trying to convince Bill to change his ways but to no avail. She pulled out the O'Malley photo album she had made when we lived next door. She even had pictures from the times the Henschkes visited us in North Carolina after we moved there. We turned to a page that held a single Christmas card as the doorbell rang.

"I can't read this card. It always makes me so sad," Mrs. Henschke said as she went to answer the back door.

Helen leaned in to us and whispered, "I bet that card is from Mom. We have to read it!"

She pulled the lining back from the album, gently lifted the card out of the book, and read aloud.

Dear Ernie and Jean,

Hope this finds you well. Ginny usually writes the cards, but she wanted me to write them for her. This Christmas is going to have special meaning for us. She is home from the hospital, but things aren't looking good for her. Please keep her in your prayers. Jack and Nancy will be home in a couple of days, so everyone will be here.

Merry Christmas, and I will keep you both informed.

Love,

Kenny

When Helen finished reading the Christmas card, we were all in tears. Mrs. Henschke walked into the room and sensed our somber mood.

"Girls, you read the card?" She looked at each of us and got teary-eyed herself. "Your mother was such a beautiful lady inside and out. She would be so proud of all of you. I can see her in all of your faces. I can especially see it in the picture I took of you girls at Megan's wedding." She walked over to the coffee table and picked up the framed picture of us with Mr. Henschke.

"I can remember when you kids came over to the house after you found out you were moving to North Carolina. Gosh, I think that was like in 1975 or '76. Ernie told your Dad that you all couldn't move. We were devastated. Ginny was great about keeping in touch with us and sharing everything going on in your lives, though. I still miss her very much."

Helen looked at her watch. "Mrs. Henschke, we have to go pick up our friend from O'Hare."

Mrs. Henschke nodded and stood. "Thank you so much for coming by. You made an old lady very happy."

"How old are you, Mrs. Henschke?" I asked as we walked out the door.

"Ninety-one," she said proudly.

"Man, I hope I look as good as you do now when I'm fifty," I said.

"You won't," Fiona assured me. We all laughed, and I punched Fiona in the arm to show her my appreciation for her comment. Mrs. Henschke walked us out to the driveway and gave us each a hug. "Thank you so much for stopping by. You'll never know how much it means to me. Jack and Murphy have stopped by to see me, and I like when it's a surprise. Tell the boys hello, and Shamus owes me a visit."

We got into the car, and I turned around to watch her walk back to her house. Memories I didn't even know I had came back to me in that moment. I had gone back in time, to a different place, a time of innocence. This place in time didn't have any illness. What it did have was endless possibilities for each of us kids. And most importantly, it had an abundance of motherly love. I turned to face the road ahead and realized our past was leading us to the future.

Chapter Twelve
Keep Going

"Can we go by St. Stephens? I want to see if I can remember the way we walked to school every day," I begged.

"Okay, but we have to make it quick if we still want to grab a bite to eat before we pick up Suson," Fiona agreed.

I was surprised at how much I actually remembered about the path we walked to school every day, considering I was only five years old at the time. Back in 1974, everyone walked to school. We had one car, and Dad used it for work. Even though I was in kindergarten, I walked three miles every day to and from school. In the morning I walked with my brothers and sister, but on the way home I walked with a boy named Mikey Olen since kindergarten was only half a day. We both were in Mrs. Pokinghorn's class. On our first day walking home together, he insisted we go a different way than what my mom had told me. We were at a busy intersection, and he said to go left. I was determined that we were to go straight. I left him crying at that corner because he wouldn't come with me. Mom was anxiously waiting for me on the front stoop with Fiona when I got home. I think I was an hour late, but I remember Mom saying that I did the right thing. She called Mikey's mom and told her what had happened. I found out later that when his mother went to the intersection, he was in the same spot, still crying and with soiled pants. From that day on he always listened to me, and we never had another problem.

The school was just as I had remembered except for the fact that it had a completely different name. Instead of St. Stephens, it was now called Our Lady of Destiny. Fiona parked the car, and we looked into the windows of the church. I thought about the funeral that the whole school had attended when I was in second grade. Helen's best friend Kathy Malloy, died of leukemia at age nine. Helen spent a lot of time with her, but they always played at Kathy's house. Helen said it had something to do with her blood count. She couldn't be exposed to germs. Fiona and I listened to her as she talked.

We walked around to the office of the elementary school where the staff was working. We explained that we had attended school there in the '70s, and they let us walk around since the school had closed for the summer.

We went down the first grade hallway and found ourselves walking into the back of the church. As we entered, Fiona stopped. Big rocks were placed everywhere at the foot of the altar. I had never seen rocks on a Catholic alter. By the looks on Fiona's and Helen's faces, I'm pretty sure they hadn't either. Being that we had collected the rocks for Mom's grave only the day before, it was a surreal moment for all of us. We looked at each other, and without saying a word, we walked over to the kneelers, lit a votive memorial candle, and all said a silent prayer.

After we left the church, we walked through the hallways of the school. I kept thinking of my best friend Annie Clark. Every day she would play with her skirt zipper, and it would catch her skin. Mrs. Pokinghorn would have to stop class and help her. I remembered the talent show we attended where three girls sang the *Captain and Tennille* song, "Love Will Keep Us Together." I thought about my brother Murphy helping nuns that worked at the school deliver lunch to our classroom every day. Just walking down the hallways of the school was like walking back in time. It felt good, comforting, like an old shoe. I thought about Jack's friend, Steve Emmanuel, who I had a huge crush on when I was in kindergarten. He wore these big glasses with black frames and even bigger lenses, but he always said "hi" to me when he came to the house.

We left the school and decided we had just enough time to grab a bite to eat before we picked up Suson Fuson at the airport. We drove down the street and found a diner that didn't look too busy.

Helen said, "Hmmm, four cars in the parking lot could mean two things: The service is fast, or it's not a good restaurant." We took our chances and walked inside since our options were limited—eat or not eat. So we sat at the 1950s-style counter and ordered three waters, while we studied the menu. Fiona sat in the middle, with Helen on her right and me on her left.

"Helen, you have to tell me the story about Colleen losing her shoes. You said you'd tell us when you saw us," I mentioned, debating the merits of the club sandwich versus the veggie burger.

"Fiona, did I tell you that Colleen has lost like five pairs of shoes?"

"No, how does she lose her shoes?" asked Fiona, surveying the menu. "I'm definitely having the tuna platter with fruit." She put the menu down on the counter.

"I don't know, but I know how she lost one pair, and they were mine. Anyway, Maggie and I went to buy some nice flip-flops at Payless last week because we have lost all of ours. Colleen is on a peer jury team at the downtown courthouse for school, and she has to get dressed up every Wednesday night. So against my better judgment, I let her borrow my heels. They aren't really high heels, nothing special, but I wear them a lot. Anyway, after she borrowed them, I kept seeing one of them in the van, and I told Colleen over and over to take the shoes in the house, so we didn't lose them. I never actually *saw* the other shoe, but I assumed it was in the back of the van somewhere, you know? So, the other day I was dropping Colleen and Casey off at school. I don't drive directly up to the school; I just let them out by this grassy area, and they walk the rest of the way. So, Colleen gets out of the car, pulls a shoe out of the grass, and says, 'I found it!' She was so relieved and proud of herself because she had been avoiding the issue for days. She just threw it back in the car and said, 'Gotta go, Mom.'

"You guys, I saw that shoe in the grass for like four days and never knew it was mine." Helen was totally disgusted and frustrated with her kids, but Fiona and I couldn't stop laughing.

The service and food were pretty good, but the best part of that meal was the fact that the three of us were just sitting together and eating lunch. So much of our time is spent talking on the phone and sending e-mails, giving each other updates about our lives, kids, and work. But I realized how happy I was to be with the two people that know me the best; the two people that have suffered the same loss and pain; the same two people that have been with me during crucial moments from high school and college graduations to my wedding and the birth of children. Just being in the same place—talking or not saying anything at all—was so peaceful. I could just be me and know they love me, no matter what. We will always have each other's support and strength. As I picked up my sandwich and took a bite, I turned my head to the right and looked at my sisters.

I'm eating lunch with Helen and Fiona, and I almost feel giddy inside because we are together.

Chapter Thirteen

Welcome to the Party

"Guys, I just got a text from Suson. She's at the lower level of the baggage claim next to the Hertz sign, wearing a blue sweater and carrying a red suitcase," Fiona informed us.

We all laugh out loud. "Helen, take note. This is how it's supposed to be when we pick you up at the airport."

"You guys are jerks," Helen sighs.

When we arrived at the airport, Suson Fuson was exactly where she said she was going to be. It was like night and day when compared to picking up Helen. Suson saw us before we saw her, and she hurried toward the car.

"Hello, O'Malley sisters! How is everybody? Megan, I love the straight hair. Fiona, I brought you a little something for driving all of us."

"Thanks, Suson Fuson!" Fiona exclaimed as she gratefully put the package Suson had given her on the console of the car.

Suson put her luggage in the back and hopped in the back seat next to Helen. Fiona shifted the car into drive. We were now just three hours away from our final destination of Dubuque, Iowa.

"Helen, how are you? You look great! Still roller-blading everyday, huh? How do you have time? Every time I talk to you, you have fifty million things going on, and Tim is gone all the time on business. How *do* you do it?" Before Helen could even answer, Suson had moved on to the next question.

"Okay, talk to me girls, what have I missed?"

We caught Suson Fuson up to speed on everything she had missed so far. From the rock collecting to Bill the Womanizer, we talked non-stop for almost two hours. Suson was laughing and hanging on to every word. Fiona was doing most of the talking when she noticed that Helen and I were buried in tabloid magazines. Fiona immediately blurted out, "We lost Helen in the back seat to the *People* and *Us Weekly* magazines. Suson, you know you can't give Helen or Megan those magazines! They get so wrapped up in them, and I can't get them back. Now, Megan comes out of it faster because she only looks at the pictures, but Helen? She's gone."

"Guys, I promise after this magazine, I'm putting them down," Helen promised. "Oh my gosh, Kim Kardashian is getting married? Hasn't she been dating that guy for like *two weeks*? That is so going to end badly. Are you kidding? Why is Bradley Cooper dating *her*? Suson, that reminds me of *The Hangover*. Last year, we went to Fiona's house, and we watched that movie probably ten times and laughed so hard. Maybe it was the wine, but that movie is *so* funny. The best part is when they wake up, and they don't know what happened or where they are, and then they find the tiger in the bathroom. It was *hilarious*," Helen said as she continued to flip the pages of the magazine.

"We watched it over and over because there was a blizzard. Remember we were supposed to see Rascal Flatts, but it was cancelled due to that snowstorm? So we just drank wine and coffee for two days and went sleigh riding. Spa Day was fun; luckily we got that in before the flippin' blizzard. The sleigh riding was fun, too, but it was so cold that day! It felt like someone was slapping my legs as hard as they could, the wind was so cold. That's one thing I don't miss about living up here. I don't think I could ever come back to those cold winters. What about you, Helen, do you think you could handle the winters again?" I ask her.

"Definitely, I would move here in a heartbeat to get out of *Florida*," Helen replied as she turned the pages of *People*.

"Wait a minute…aren't you the one who loses your toenails every time you come home to Ohio at Thanksgiving and run the Turkey Trot because of the cold weather? And don't your fingertips turn white when you're in the air conditioning too long?" I inquire as I scan the pictures of my magazine, not making eye contact.

"I would just have to get used to it again," Helen said very seriously.

"Riiiiiiiiiight," I say sarcastically. We all chuckle.

These trips are our lifelines to one another. We could schedule a couple of days in a funeral home, and as long as we have coffee, wine, and each other, we're good. Suson asks about the itinerary for the weekend and whom she will be meeting.

"Okay, tonight you're going to meet Uncle John, who is Mom's little brother, and he will probably be at the hotel when we get there. Aunt Kitty, Mom's sister, and her husband, Uncle Dick, will be coming later and maybe bringing our cousin Kathy. Funny side bar: Aunt Kitty and Uncle Dick have seven kids—two girls and five boys. The boys' names are John, Danny, Michael, Dick, and Tom. Since my uncle and his son have the same name, there was always confusion when someone called their house. When people would call on the phone, they would ask for Dick. So the person who answered would respond nonchalantly, 'Big Dick or Little Dick?'" Fiona had us laughing until we cried.

When we gathered ourselves, she continued. "Okay, and then we have Aunt Joni who was married to Uncle Frank, Mom's oldest brother, who passed away about five years ago. She might come to the hotel but will definitely be at dinner. Our Uncle Frank was basically a legend at Walhert High School in Dubuque. Actually, I think they re-named the gym after him. He was the basketball coach and a history teacher for forty years at the school. He started out as the assistant coach but eventually became the head coach. I'm pretty sure they won like ten state tournaments. Jack and Murphy went to his funeral mass that was held in the school gym, and it was standing room only."

I turned around and directed my question to Helen, "Didn't he play professional baseball, or he was drafted right out of high school? For some reason, I want to say the team in Chicago, is that the Red Sox or the White Sox? No wait, I'm pretty sure it was the Milwaukee Brewers, but Grandpa Delany said he couldn't play until he finished his education."

"Yeah, I think you're right, Meg, but I don't know what happened. We need to ask Uncle John. He'll know."

"Girls, I don't know a lot about sports, but I do know that the Red Sox are in St. Louis and the White Sox are in Chicago," said Suson very confidently. "Pete's a big fan of baseball."

"Didn't Aunt Joni send you guys that article in the *Telegraph Herald* about Uncle Frank?" Fiona asked, fiddling with the radio and trying to keep her eyes on the road.

"She did, but I haven't read it since she sent it to us like four or five years ago," Helen replied.

"Yeah, me either. I need to read it again. Hey, did I ever tell you guys the story about meeting one of his students after church a long time ago?" I added.

"What are you talking about? You mean you met one of his students in Charleston?"

"Yeah, I was about eight months pregnant with Seth, and I left mass after communion because I was starving. When I was walking to my car, I noticed a license plate from Dubuque, so I waited until they came to their car."

"This will be good," Fiona said sarcastically. The girls smirked.

"I think Fiona's right; this is going to be embarrassing for you, Meg," Helen said.

"So, I'm waiting for church to end, and as people are walking to their cars, they all keep asking me if I'm okay because I'm huge, and it's like a hundred and twenty degrees out. I'm just standing there looking like an idiot. The longer I wait, the more determined I am to find out if they knew any of the Delanys. Finally this cute couple walks toward the car.

"So, I approach them and introduce myself so they don't think—well I don't know what they were thinking—but anyway, I asked them if they had lived in Dubuque for a long time. The woman was really nice and told me they had three boys, grown and married, and they had lived in Dubuque their whole lives. She had gone to St. Mary's college and knew Mom, Uncle

Frank had taught all of their boys, and two of them played on his basketball team. Her husband came over to us after we had been talking for about fifteen minutes. He knew Grandpa Delany and had worked at Metz Furniture Store back when Grandpa was president of the company. They were the nicest people and invited me to have brunch with them."

"Did you go?"

"No, I said good-bye, apologized for taking up their time, and told them to have a great vacation. But, I got a phone call from Aunt Joni about three weeks later telling me she and Uncle Frank were at a viewing at some funeral home and ran into this couple that I had met! Of course, they had nothing but pleasant things to say, you know, about me."

"That actually is pretty cool, Meg," Helen responded. "But sometimes you talk to people about nothing, and it gets you in trouble. Remember my high school reunion that you and Fiona came to?"

"No, we are not talking about that."

Suson piped up, "What happened? Meggy, come on, tell Suson what happened."

Fiona turned the radio down and simplified the story. "Megan and Helen came into Dayton for Helen's twenty-fifth high school reunion...remember you couldn't come for some reason? Anyway, we told her we would stop by for about an hour, but after that, we were out of there. So while Helen is talking to people, Megan and I were on our own. Megan, didn't you tell that guy that you were on the cross country team?""

I giggle. "Okay, Suson, in my defense, he was really cute, and he recognized me, so I just went with it," I said.

"Megan, I ran cross county, you idiot," Helen yelled from the back seat. "He thought you were me!"

"He asked if I was still running, and I told him I was running a seven-minute mile," I said. "Actually, I couldn't run if my life depended on it. Anyway, a couple of years ago, I got this book from a former teacher's wife from high school. The book was a kindergarten workbook, and I took it to school to show other teachers and see if it was something we could use, but they decided it was too expensive. Since we never used it, I gave it to a parent to work with her child at home, you know, for like extra practice. Anyway, as I'm talking to this teacher, I didn't know what to say, so I tell him I really liked his wife's kindergarten workbook. He insisted that I meet her. I've had a couple of drinks, so I'm thinking, *what the heck?* We had like ten minutes before our required hour of attendance was up. I decide I'm going to make this lady's day by telling her how great her book is. She introduces herself and asks me how I used her workbook. I took a sip of my drink and said, 'We used it in small groups.'

"She replies, 'How many workbooks do you have at your school?'

"I start to panic because I'm not sure where she is going with this, so I take a sip of my drink and say, 'One?'

"Her smile just melts off her face, and she leans in to me, shaking her finger, and says with disgust, 'So, you make copies of the one book?'

"'Um,' I take another sip of my drink and reply, 'yes?' I didn't know what she was getting at and all I could think was, *where the hell are Helen and Fiona?*

"She gives me a look that bores into my soul and says, 'So you're stealing from me. That's just great! I'm in litigation with some people right now because they have stolen it, too. So we have a problem.'

"I didn't even know how to respond to what she was saying to me. All I kept thinking was that she was going to take me to court over something I have never done. I was trying to make her feel good about her stupid book, that's it. I started looking everywhere for Helen and Fiona because I knew we needed to get out of there pronto."

Fiona interjects into the story, "On the other side of the room, I saw the look on Megan's face and said to Helen, 'Megan's in trouble. We have to go help!'"

"So Fiona and Helen came out of nowhere and started talking, introducing themselves and even taking pictures to distract this couple. After a couple of minutes, they got me out of there, and we walked directly to the car. When we got inside, I explained what happened. Fiona laughs like a mad woman, and Helen is just in total disbelief and says, 'Megan, you have to think about what you say! You are such an idiot. Good thing Jack is an attorney because it sounds like you're going to need one!'"

"Megan, did she ever press charges?" Suson asked.

"My attorney says I'm not allowed to discuss anything right now," I said with a straight face.

"Holy shit, Meg, you've got to be kidding!"

I turned around, looked her straight in the eye, and said, "I am."

We all cracked up.

"Okay, guys, I'm stopping at this exit up here because I have to go to the bathroom. I might get a snack or two. Do you guys mind?" Fiona asks, switching lanes.

"Nope, not at all. I need a snack. I haven't eaten anything, and I'm starving," said Suson.

Fiona pulls up to the gas station, and we all walk inside. I stop on one aisle, and everyone else follows to peek over my shoulder.

"What are you looking for?" Suson inquires as she turns to go to the restroom.

"Nothing," I say, "Just looking."

I headed over to the deli and ordered a twelve-inch veggie sub. Then I made my way back through the aisles until I found what I needed. I picked up the blue package, grabbed my sub, and headed to the register without anyone noticing.

Out of nowhere, Fiona walks up to the counter and adds some gum to my bill.

"Okay, let me get this straight, you're buying a twelve-inch sub and *fiber pills*?" She looked at me incredulously.

"I didn't have time to go this morning! We left at four-forty, and I'm just trying to help things move along...."

"You don't think that fifteen-foot sandwich is going to do some moving?"

"Shut up! Do you want me to buy your gum or not?"

"Okay, but if that pill starts working before we get to the hotel, you're walking the rest of the way."

"Whatever." I wince.

"Hey, Megan, can you buy something for dizziness? I feel carsick," Helen said.

"Maybe you should stop reading those magazines? Hello, don't you think that is doing something to your head? There are a lot of curves and turns on this road," I retort.

"Actually Megan, you might need those magazines to help your situation, if you know what I mean. Turn *good news* into *bad news*. Get it, take *good news* and turn it into *bad news*. Get my drift?" Fiona laughs when she says "good news...bad news."

"You're such an idiot! Just because Mom always called a bowel movement 'bad news' doesn't mean you can get away with it!" I tease her.

"What's the problem?" Helen asks, joining us.

"Megan's constipated," Fiona gasps through her laughter.

"Shut up! Quit talking so loud," I scold. Suson yells out from the back of the store, "Megan, if you need some Phillips, I packed some."

"Really, guys? Thanks." I roll my eyes and check out. "Okay, come on, I'm ready. Uncle John is waiting for us at the hotel, and I have a feeling these fiber pills are going to get things moving. Let's roll."

After an hour, we cross over the Mississippi River, and we all feel relief that we have finally arrived at our destination. Helen's head is ready to burst, along with her stomach. Suson needs a cigarette. Fiona is exhausted, and I need not explain what I'm feeling. Yes, the fiber pills are working. Fiona throws the directions to me as she opens the window and gives me a not-so-kind look.

"I can't help it!" I say, laughing. The two back windows go down as well. "I think we turn on Main Street, right?" I try to pretend like I don't notice what they are doing, but the smell is starting to make me sick, too.

"Now make a left here and then another left," I instructed Fiona.

"Hey, there's the hotel on the right. Where is the parking lot?" Helen asks.

"What the hell did you eat, Megan? That's repulsive!" Suson yells from the back seat.

"I think this is a perfect time for me to hop out and get us checked in."

Chapter Fourteen
Hello, Stranger

"I 'll call you and tell you where the room is. I've got Helen's luggage," I say as I hop out of the car.

"Seriously? You are on your own with that trunk you've got in the back," Helen objects.

"It's The Collection, my friends. Technically it's *everybody's* luggage." I grab Helen's Hello Kitty backpack and quickly close the car door before they can give me any lip. I jog into the Julian Hotel. The lobby is gorgeous with marble floors and floral arrangements everywhere. I take a couple of deep breaths and breathe in the pleasant aroma to clear my olfactory senses. To my left is a grand stairway leading to the second floor rooms, and to my right is a quaint sitting area with a leather sofa and two reading chairs. There is a computer area for the guests to use, along with chairs and tables for cozy conversations and cocktails that overlook Main Street. In the middle of the room, a round sofa encircles a huge floral arrangement. It's beautiful. I think how gorgeous that plant would be in my stairway by the bay window at my house. Then I start to wonder why I don't have pretty plants at my house. *Oh, I know why. I can barely keep up with dusting off my plants, let alone watering them. That plant would be serving a death sentence if it ever got to my house. I guess I will stick to the plastic kind.*

Anyway, as I'm walking to the front desk, I look ahead and notice a man pacing back and forth, jingling change in his pockets. At first I don't recognize him because the huge floral arrangement is blocking his face. Suddenly, a memory of my Grandpa Delany walking back and forth, waiting for us to get

100

ready at his house, flooded my mind. It's my Uncle John. I rush over to him. We hug and examine each other since we haven't seen each other in eight years.

"Uncle John! You look great!" I compliment my mother's youngest brother.

He says, "Not bad for an old man with one foot in the grave, huh? Where is everybody?"

"They're parking the car if they can find the parking lot. They dropped me off out front. I'm supposed to check us in and then give them directions to the room."

"Well then, let's get you checked in, little lady."

He walks me to the front desk, and I check into room 428.

"Ma'am, how many keys would you like?"

"Two would be great, if that's okay?"

"My pleasure, Mrs. Moller, will there be anything else that I can do for you?"

"Where is the nearest bar?" Uncle John bursts out laughing beside me.

"Most certainly, go down these stairs and to your right you will see the restaurant. It's called Julian's, and the bar is located inside."

"Great, thanks," I pick up the keys and my information about the hotel. Uncle John and I head towards the bar. We descend two flights of stairs, and I notice the parking area right outside the door.

"Uncle John, I'm going try and call them, if you don't mind. I should probably tell them where we are."

"Sounds good. We're gonna need somebody to pay for our tab."

"I'm one step ahead of you!" I say as I give him a wink.

I dial each of the girls in turn, but I don't get an answer from anyone.

"No one is answering. Let's just head in," I nod to Uncle John to lead the way. I put my phone back in my purse while he holds the door for me. I catch him eyeing my bright pink Hello Kitty backpack, but he doesn't say anything. "Uncle John, how is Aunt Pat doing?" I haven't seen his wife in ages.

"Pat's getting along just fine. She complained a bit of a migraine yesterday and today, so she's home, resting."

"That's too bad. It would have been nice to see her! What time is Aunt Kitty coming?"

"Around five-thirty. She is bringing Kathy and Uncle Dick."

"Great! That gives us time to catch up. How is it that you never age, Uncle John? I can't believe you're seventy!"

"Good genes, I guess. Wait, that can't be it, can it?"

He gave me a mischievous grin, and we both giggled awkwardly. My grandmother died eight days after giving birth to Uncle John from a blood clot as a result of not getting out of bed. So simple, yet so tragic; something that could have been prevented. She was only thirty-two years old and had four other children at home—ages five, four, three, and two. My mom never had any memories of her own mother since she was only two when my grandmother died. All my mother and her siblings had of her was a picture. Grandpa kept a beautiful black and white photo of Grandma displayed on the coffee table in the living room. She was lovely in her light-colored chiffon blouse with tiny roses, angelic skin, and chestnut brown hair pulled back gently at the base of her neck. I was always most fascinated with her eyes. They were warm and inviting and seemed as if they could tell a thousand stories of courage and inspiration.

The bar is empty and apparently closed, but the bartender notices us and wants to accommodate. He opens the door. "Do you have dinner reservations?" He inquires.

"No, we're just here for the bar, if that's okay," I say sheepishly.

"The restaurant doesn't open until five, but I'll be happy to serve you two," the bartender insists, ushering us inside. "Bob," he introduces himself as he places napkins in front of us. "What can I get for you?"

"I'll have a bourbon and water," Uncle John says.

"Do you have Guinness on tap?" I ask.

"Sure."

"Okay, great, that's what I will have then please. Can you also tell me where the ladies room is?"

"Go around the bar and to your right."

"Thanks. I'll be right back, Uncle John."

When I came back, my drink and Uncle John were waiting for me. It wasn't uncomfortable, but I hadn't seen my uncle in eight years. This was really the first time as an adult I was talking with him one-on-one. When we saw each other in the past, we usually just exchanged small talk. My older brothers dominated the conversation, and I didn't have a whole lot to say, although Helen and Fiona would beg to differ. However, I knew three important facts about this man.

My mother adored her little brother. He always says, "A good bug is a dead bug." (Living in South Carolina where our state bird is a cockroach, I can appreciate this guy on a level most people can't.) And most importantly, he always makes me smile.

We toasted each other with our drinks as Fiona, Helen, and Suson walked into the bar dragging our luggage, including my huge suitcase.

"Hello, you were supposed to call us, Megan?" Fiona admonished me.

"I did call! Uncle John, tell them. None of you answered." Uncle John laughs as he begins to realize he might have his hands full with us for the next twenty-four hours. Fiona and Suson walk toward me as Helen struggles with The Collection. "I got a little distracted," I say and take a sip of my beer. I extend my pinky finger like I am royalty. "And I had to use the facilities when I arrived, so that took a little time, too."

"Thank goodness for small miracles. Now if I could only get that stench out of my car. Uncle John, can you believe we have to put up with her?" Fiona teases.

"Hi, girls!" Uncle John pushes back his bar stool and embraces Helen and Fiona. Their hugs are long and sincere.

"Uncle John, this is our friend Suson Fuson."

"Hi, John, can I call you Uncle John?"

"Sure. So you are with these wise guys, huh?"

"Yep, they're cheap entertainment," Suson assures him.

"I can only imagine…."

During all of this, the bartender is moving all of the suitcases against the corner wall of the bar. He places the pink Hello Kitty backpack on the top, eyeing it strangely. I don't think Bob the Bartender has been this busy in years. He places napkins in front of the girls, taking their drink orders.

"I'll have a chardonnay," Suson says. Fiona orders a Michelob Ultra, and Helen asks for a cabernet.

"Okay, guys, we need a picture! Everybody smile!" Fiona hands her camera to Bob, and he walks around the bar to capture our moment.

Suson steps out to check her messages, Fiona runs to the front desk to buy cigarettes, (she promised it was the last pack), and Helen rustles through her purse to find her Burt's Bees.

I ask Bob if he has any snacks.

He pulls out bowls of peanuts and Chex Mix for us.

"You know, yesterday when I was flying from Atlanta to Dayton, they announced that rows seventeen through twenty-one weren't allowed to have peanuts because there was a peanut allergy in one of those rows." I informed everyone as I was munching down.

"Really?" Suson asks loudly. Her inquiry catches everyone's attention. Now I have four people, maybe five, if you include Bob, staring at me.

"Yep, and the people in rows seventeen through twenty-one got a cookie that tasted like cotton. I seriously wanted to find some peanuts and throw them in rows twenty and twenty-one."

"Why those aisles?" Uncle John asks.

"Because I was the only person in row seventeen, and no one was in eighteen or nineteen, so the allergy person was in either twenty or twenty-one."

Bob listens closely and looks me straight in the eye, drying cocktail glasses, and says, "You're mean." He had gotten the memo that we were a fun group and he could joke with us.

"I got two things for you, " I eagerly respond, returning his look. "Number one: That is so going to affect your tip." We all laugh, including Bob. "And number two: I hadn't eaten all day, and I was starving for a little something with substance. Out of everyone on the whole plane, only like four people got the stupid cookie that gave you cotton mouth. It should have been all or nothing. Either give everybody the cookie or don't give anything at all. Why just those rows? What would happen if the allergy person used the bathroom, and it was located on a peanut aisle? Or if a peanut eater touched something and then the allergy person touched it, and it had traces of peanut? This was not thought through very well at all, and the person must not have had that bad of an allergy. I don't understand why I had to be inconvenienced. You see where I'm going here? It doesn't make sense."

"Ah, yes. We get it. You *are* mean!" Bob retorts.

We all cackle.

The stories started flowing. In addition to Bob, the rest of the wait staff hung around the end of the bar to hear them. Fiona told us later that she heard one waitress say that the bar hadn't seen this much life in years. We talked for about an hour before Aunt Kitty showed up with Uncle Dick and Kathy. We ordered more drinks, and Bob worked his tail off.

Uncle John pulled out a photo album filled with pictures of Mom, Aunt Kitty, Uncle Frank, my aunt Myrna, and him. He propped it right up on the bar, and he and Aunt Kitty relived stories of their past. I could tell Bob was trying to figure out our odd group because I saw him leaning over the bar, focusing on a picture of Mom. He then turned to look at Helen and Fiona. I suppose it's because they look a lot like her. Lucky ducks.

Looking at the photos, I was surprised at how much my Ginny looks like Mom did when she was younger. *They have the same eyes,* I thought to myself. I wish Mom could have met Tom and the kids. I wish they could have heard the stories that Aunt Kitty and Uncle John were telling of her. Part of me was forlorn because I kept imagining Mom sitting here with us, drinking her Manhattan and laughing and enjoying every minute with her brother and sister. She had a way of bringing sunshine inside the darkest of places, a way of brightening up the people she was around. I miss her even more when I'm with John and Kitty because I see her in them. For the longest time after she died, I couldn't even look at Aunt Kitty without crying. In my eyes, she was the closest thing we had to Mom. I sobbed like a child when I saw her walk into the hotel for my wedding rehearsal dinner. Seeing her emphasized the void of not having my mother with me. I have many memories of Mom and Aunt Kitty together— holidays, family football games, visits to my grandpa's house— she was always there with her family. She and Mom would be in the kitchen cooking, cleaning, or preparing the next meal. Laughter was a staple in that kitchen, even when they were busy cooking for twenty people. They were best friends; the way sisters should be. Maybe that's why my sisters and I find so much comfort in one another. We learned from their example.

Chapter Fifteen

The Line Up

U ncle Dick and Uncle John split our bar tab. We needed to leave in order to make our seven-thirty dinner reservations at Timmerman's Restaurant. Uncle John informed us that we were riding with him since he knew the way. We walked out to the car, and Helen climbed in the front seat. Fiona, Suson, and I hopped in the back. As we drove back over the bridge, Uncle John gave us a few words about East Dubuque. He said, "Don't go. Crime is high, and the drugs are rampant." That's all we needed to know.

We pulled into the parking lot, and I immediately remembered being there with my grandpa when I was younger. Grandpa Delany would always take us to Timmerman's for dinner on special occasions when we came into town. Growing up with six kids in the family, going out to dinner was a rarity and always a treat. The restaurant was known for its fresh catfish from the Mississippi River, but the best part of the experience was the view.

Timmerman's is located on top of a cliff that has sweeping views of the river. It has a fenced-in area for wildlife right outside the windows of the main private dining area. And by "wildlife," I mean rabbits.

The hostess seated us at our table. Uncle Frank's widow, Aunt Joni, met us there. We sat at a large, round table overlooking the river a hundred feet below us. The sunset over the water was breathtaking. Uncle John pulled out my chair for me, and I sat next to him. The men debated over the bill for a while, finally deciding that Uncle John would pay the liquor bill, and Uncle

Dick would pay the meal bill. Once they straightened that out, we ordered drinks.

Helen and Fiona were engrossed in a conversation with Aunt Kitty, and my attention was primarily on Uncle John. I did not realize the impact my mother's death had on him until that night. She was a little mother to him although she was only two years older. "She was my biggest fan, and I think about her every day," he said.

He told me about her convincing him to go to a dance once in high school. "I didn't want to go, but she made it sound so great because the after party was so much fun. She and your dad were going to be there, too. So I asked a girl to go with me, was grilled by her parents, and went to the dance. My date's mother informed me when I went to pick her up that after the dance, we were to come home immediately, and they would have sandwiches for us. It was a terrible night." He chuckled. "I never got to the after party, but I never stopped taking advice from your mom."

I told him how guilty I felt about all the things I didn't do for my mom when she was alive and how Fiona and Helen and Tom insisted that visiting her grave was my opportunity to move forward. I vowed, "I'm leaving all of it at the grave tomorrow. I just have to let it go. I'm so glad that you will be with us. Fiona has scheduled a spa day for us afterwards because we know we are going to need it." Uncle John listened intently and nodded.

I continued, "Fiona and I collected rocks the other night for everybody in our family, including you. By placing the rocks on Mom's grave, we're leaving behind a little piece of us." I paused for a moment and took a sip of my wine, placed my napkin on the table, and wiped away some crumbs from my lap. Then I rested my elbows on the table, leaned in toward him, and said, "You know you're going to have a lot to deal with tomorrow? I was a psych major for two weeks. We are going to need serious help." He winked at me and smiled.

Suson jumped between Fiona's conversation and mine. For not knowing anyone but us, she did great. She ordered her chardonnay and kept up with both conversations. I think the highlight of the night was when Uncle Dick told us about his photo shoot with the football great, Kurt Warner. He had just gotten back from Phoenix where the shoot was done for Scholastic Books. Uncle Dick was Mr. Warner's football coach at Regis High School in Cedar Rapids, Iowa. Mr. Warner had made it known that my uncle was a big influence on him as a teacher and a coach. The slogan had something to do with how important teachers are, and Uncle Dick was thrilled when Mr. Warner approached him about it.

Aunt Kitty initiated our departure after dinner. We walked out to the parking lot, and Fiona said we needed to take a group picture. Since no one had a camera, my cousin Kathy offered her cell phone. Suson assumed the job of official photographer, and we all posed. The first picture was all of us lined up turned to the right facing the same direction. It looked like a line up. So to mix it up, we turned the other way and took another picture. Fiona said we should do something crazy for the last one, and we wound up looking like a bunch of cheerleaders. It was like one of those Kodak commercials when they mention the material price, but the emotional factor at the end is priceless.

Our Trip to Dubuque
Three airline tickets: $867.00
Nine dinners: $375.00
Liquor bill for the entire weekend: $ridiculousness
Group picture of my aunts and uncles doing a line up pose:
Priceless

We arrived back at the Julian Hotel, and the girls got glasses of wine from Bartender Bob before we headed up to Uncle John's room. I think Bob was sad that we didn't stick around to entertain him.

Uncle John's room was tidy and untouched. He reminded me of Helen because he packed so lightly. He put his backpack on the bed and pulled out one clean shirt and a huge bottle of Black

Velvet Bourbon. I had never seen such a big bottle of liquor. We O'Malleys take our Irish heritage seriously. I realized then that Uncle John reminded me more of a big brother than an uncle.

We looked at his photo albums, and he told us about the dude ranch he and Aunt Kitty had visited in Montana. They stayed for a week, just the two of them, and worked on the ranch after Aunt Kitty's daughter, my cousin Sara Beth, died of breast cancer. We cracked up when he told us about the chuck wagon, which held all of the food supplies. He referred to the "real cowboy" with the utmost respect. He also talked about the "young guns," who were only teenagers or maybe a little older and could handle any task on the ranch.

Uncle John told us that when he rode his horse at any kind of speed, his hat would fly off his head. So he pulled the cord attached to his hat and tightened it around his chin. However when the "young guns," started to ride faster, his horse picked up speed as well. His hat blew off and the cord twisted tightly around his neck, choking him. As he was trying to signal Aunt Kitty, his saddle started slipping. He had one leg on the horse's back and his other leg under the horse. Kitty's horse ran ahead trying to keep the pace of the other horses, so Uncle John was on his own. He held on for about a half a mile before the horse slowed down. When the horse finally came to a complete stop, his front and back feet were in a huge mud puddle. Uncle John let go and fell straight into the middle of the puddle. Everyone laughed at him, and he said he could have sworn that the horse was laughing at him, too. "If I had a gun, I would have shot that stupid horse between the ears," he told us.

We told stories until the wee hours in the morning. I kept fading in and out because my eyelids were so heavy, but the laughter always brought me back. I didn't want to miss a minute of the conversation, but I was exhausted. I finally gave up the fight to stay awake and headed back to our room around one-thirty. When I look back on that night, I will always remember Uncle John wearing his cowboy boots and a contagious grin, sitting on the edge of the bed, holding his drink and talking about the dude ranch, laughing and so full of life.

Chapter Sixteen
A New Perspective

We awoke the next morning to the phone ringing and realized we had overslept. We had thirty minutes to get ready and meet Uncle John downstairs in the lobby. Today was game day. We were going to the cemetery. Helen was looking for an outfit from The Collection, but her criteria was it had to be dark, which limited her options in my sea of summer clothing. I spied Suson using Fiona's Tough Actin' Tinactin. *Perfect, I thought, we're sharing the same double bed, and it's going to be a miracle if I make it home without my first case of athlete's foot.* Fiona was turning the room upside-down, looking for her cell phone. Our room was a complete zoo for those thirty minutes, but we made it.

When we finally got to the lobby, Uncle John was waiting for us like a schoolboy going on a field trip. He was excited and ready to go, and he offered to drive us in Fiona's car. The first stop on our tour was Grandpa Delany's house, the childhood home of Mom, Kitty, Uncle Frank, Aunt Myrna, and Uncle John. They lived on a street called Mount Pleasant, which happens to be the city in South Carolina where my family and I now live. Coincidence? I don't think so.

Grandpa Delany's house was made of stone and had dark green awnings. It looked exactly like I remembered. As we looked through the neighborhood, we noticed most of the houses were made of stone. Uncle John informed us that our great-grandfather Kolfenback had a brother with a drinking problem, and he started a cement company to keep him busy so he wouldn't have time to drink. From the number of stone houses, I would say this kid didn't have time to sleep, let alone drink.

We drove by Grandma and Grandpa O'Malley's house on Long Grove, my dad's childhood home. We made our way past Bunker Hill where we went sledding every time it snowed and passed Washington High School where we played several nail-biter touch football games with our cousins when we visited during the holidays.

After about fifteen minutes, we reached Mount Olivet Cemetery. I looked at Fiona, and she put her sunglasses on. The view from my window was beautiful. The sun was shining and the temperature was pleasant. Birds were singing, and the sky was clear, a Carolina blue that made me think twice about where I was at the time. The cemetery had rolling green hills and huge oak trees. Everything about it was peaceful and serene. I noticed the plants and wreaths left by visiting friends or relatives on several graves that we passed on the way to Mom's. I wondered had Mom been buried in a cemetery near me, would I have come religiously like these people do? *Does it get easier the more you come, or is it like experiencing the loss all over again?*

Uncle John drove a slow fifteen miles per hour on the tiny road through the cemetery. The car was silent. We anxiously looked out the window, anticipating when the car would come to a complete stop. He slowed down, pulled the car to the side of the black asphalt road, and killed the engine. This was it. I was about to see my mother's grave, the place she had been buried twenty-five years earlier. We got out and walked up the hill. I followed Uncle John with my head down, reading the names chiseled into the headstones we passed. Helen carried flowers. I looked up when Uncle John stopped walking and turned around. I knew we were there.

M. Ginny O'Malley
Sept. 20, 1938 – Dec. 25, 1985

The lump in my throat was the size of a basketball. I didn't want to start crying, but I was feeling her death all over again. The loss and emptiness I felt were overwhelming and so powerful that I couldn't control my emotions. I sobbed like a child. Uncle John put his arm around my shoulders, and I leaned into him. Fiona showed no emotion, just as she had at my mother's funeral, but I could tell she was crying. I wanted to be strong like she and Helen are, but they are made of different clay. I looked at Suson, and even though she was wearing glasses, her shaking shoulders gave away the fact that she was crying, too.

So many memories flooded my mind. When I was little, I always knew what kind of mood Mom was in when I woke up by the way the pots and pans where banging in the kitchen. She always let you know she was in a bad mood by how loudly she banged them. If they were loud, you knew to be on your best behavior. If the kitchen was quiet, you could skip making the bed before school. Mom was also the loudest parent cheering in the stands at every sporting event. She would get so fired up at the boys for eating her Christmas cookies in the freezer after football practice. She hated having her picture taken, especially after she got sick, because she thought she looked terrible. I can envision her yelling at Dad for continuously trying. The irony of the present moment was that it was almost completely silent, while Mom was always so full of life, either laughing or yelling at us kids for something silly we did. The only thing I could hear was the sound of tears.

Frankly, I was so tired of listening to the physical proof of my grief. I thought about my mother's last birthday and how she comforted me. As a mother now myself, I think back to how she tried to protect us kids from her illness. She was reassuring and positive, so we wouldn't worry about her or life without her. *Would I ever be able to do what she did if I was in a similar situation?* I escaped my thoughts for a moment and looked at Helen and Fiona. They were both deep in their own thoughts. I turned back to my mother's grave and cried even harder. *Why did you leave me?* I thought to myself. *I wasn't ready to let go yet. I needed you.*

Helen motioned to us to go get the rocks from the car. I saw her wipe a tear from her cheek. When we each had rocks in our hands, I thought about the letter that Amy had written to me. I opened the back door of the car and fumbled through my purse looking for the yellow envelope. I pulled it out, tucked it under my arm, and walked back up the hill to meet the others. Fiona laid some of the rocks around the huge tree near the graves. Grandma's and Grandpa's graves were adjacent to Mom's, and Helen placed flowers on all three.

Fiona decided that the girls' rocks needed to be around Mom's tombstone and Dad's, Uncle John's, and the boys' should be around the tree. As she secured the rocks, I pulled out my letter from Amy and started digging a hole next to my rock. Uncle John bent down and helped me by digging with Fiona's car key and fingers. The dirt was dry because it hadn't rained in weeks, which made our task more difficult. He made some silly joke to lighten the mood. I was so thankful he was there with us.

I watched as Helen compared her rock to Murphy's. I swear I could see her wondering if the size difference was intentional. I couldn't help but laugh, and that lightened the mood. The next thing I knew, Helen walked back to the car and returned with a tiny box in hand. She started digging a hole next to her rock by Mom's grave, too. Come to find out, the box held a rosary that Mom had given her for her first communion. Fiona didn't want to be left out, so she chose to bury another rock. She said she wasn't creative enough to think of anything else.

Once we had secured the rocks and buried everything we wanted to leave, we all said the Memorare, my mother's favorite prayer, out loud.

"Remember, O most gracious Virgin Mary that never was it known that anyone who fled to thy protection, implored thy help, or sought thy intercession was left unaided. Inspired with this confidence, I fly to thee, O Virgin of virgins, my Mother; to thee do I come; before thee I stand, sinful and sorrowful. O Mother of the Word Incarnate, despise not my petitions, but in thy mercy, hear and answer me. Amen."

My petition was for my mother to find a way to tell me that she loved me and that she was proud of me. I needed to know that more than anything, so I could move on and be a better wife and mother. I knew it was selfish, but I couldn't help it.

As we stood there, I thought about the words to that song, "Both Sides Now." The more I thought about it, the more I realized I had been wrong about so many things. I had been wrong about the feelings I had about my mom dying. It wasn't me, or any of us kids, or even my dad who had been cheated by life without her. It was *Mom* who had been cheated. I was baffled that it took me so long to realize this simple truth. I had to travel over eleven hundred miles, but I finally saw the light.

She was the one who was cheated. She knew she wasn't going to see her children grow up. She knew she would never meet her grandchildren or spend those special years growing old with my dad. She had to endure countless surgeries, chemo, and doctor visits, while still trying to raise a family. She didn't have time to feel sorry for herself because no one else was cooking dinner for the family or washing the laundry. (I obviously wasn't doing it right.) While she was praying her novenas to St. Theresa to be cured, she still had to go to the grocery store and worry about sending out Christmas cards.

It wasn't until that moment, looking at her grave, that it all made sense to me. She knew she was going to die, but she continued to raise her kids the best she could. She demonstrated courage, discipline, and faith better than anyone I have ever known. I came to admire her more than I ever had. Personally, I'm overwhelmed working a full-time job and running a household, often complaining I never have enough time to do the things I need to do. Yet, Mom would lay in a hospital bed getting her chemotherapy at Ohio State University Hospital for a week at a time, and upon returning home, she was too sick to eat, but she would always notice the things that needed to done around the house. I can vividly see her scrubbing our bathroom upstairs and then throwing up in the toilet because she was so sick. She would try and kneel the best she could on her left leg since her right leg never bent all the way after one of her surgeries. It was not a forgiving position, and I'm sick to my stomach thinking of what she endured for us.

My mother's memory lives on through my brothers and sisters. Shamus and Fiona have her sense of humor. They can find humor in anything. Others always want to spend more time with them because their personalities are infectious. They make life easier for the rest of us by showing us not to take ourselves so seriously, and not many people in the world can do that. This trait sets them apart, and the world is a better place because of them.

Helen and Murphy have Mom's discipline and her courage. They never say they "can't." They have always plowed right through the obstacles they have faced. When they set a goal, they are inspiring. There isn't anything they can't do, and it isn't because of their stellar educations or amazing talents; it is because they don't give up. They've had to fight for everything they have ever wanted.

Jack has my mom's confidence and intelligence. He's charming and smart, the most financially secure of all of us, and yet sincere enough to know that being a good father is more important than any amount of wealth. I will never forget his toast at Murphy's wedding. He was so eloquent and heartfelt about his relationship with our brothers. He had the crowd laughing one minute and crying the next. It was a beautiful moment.

I haven't figured out what trait I have of my mom's, but I'm wondering if putting together The Collection for the weekend can count for something? She always did have great taste. I know I'm reaching. *Someday I'll figure it out,* I think to myself.

We stayed by Mom's grave for a few more minutes before deciding we needed to stop by Uncle Frank's. Uncle John led us to the car, and we drove the short distance to the St. Joseph Chapel Mausoleum. The other mausoleums have pictures of the deceased displayed to the public. I didn't look that closely at those pictures, though, because when we arrived, we had a moment of silence for my Uncle Frank. After a minute, I noticed Uncle John looking at the neighboring couple's picture. He was in deep thought. I walked over to him, thinking he may have known the couple. But as I leaned in to him to make sure he was okay, he whispered to me, "I can guarantee you that she wore the pants in that family."

I looked at the picture and started to laugh. I knew exactly what he meant. The woman looked to be about eighty-four years old. She had short white hair and a square looking face. She appeared solid with huge hands and reminded me of a German soldier. That woman was probably a fabulous cook in her day, and she definitely didn't skip any meals. Her husband looked to be half her size, and his presence was not commanding; he looked very petite in the picture. His glasses took up his entire face, but he looked so happy with his bride. That's when I stopped laughing and thought, *how adorable.* After all the time they must have been married, he still looked so in love with his German soldier-bride. I hope my husband looks at me that way when we're that old.

We climbed into the car to head back to the hotel. As we were leaving the cemetery, I noticed the sun was hiding behind the clouds, the clear blue sky had turned hazy, and rain was drizzling on the car. It was sprinkling, almost like tears. I know it sounds crazy, but I felt like they were tears of joy from Mom. As if she was crying because her three girls and her little brother had come to visit after a very long absence. Maybe she was proud of us. *Mom continues to be a mother even from heaven,* I think to myself.

I realized how important it was for us to share this trip with my mother's siblings. This trip wasn't just about my mother or my sisters or me. It was about family. It brought us together and made us realize how lucky we are to have each other, even if we are separated by air and land. We will always be connected to each other. As we were leaving, Uncle John said, "Ginny would be having so much fun if she was here." I knew he was right.

Chapter Seventeen

Ve-git-a-bul

We left the cemetery and went to breakfast to gather our thoughts. We had some time before we needed to get back to the hotel for our spa day. After bagels and several cups of coffee, we decided we'd go to Galena, Illinois.

Galena is a cute historic town that is nestled in the hills of Northwest Illinois. It hadn't changed a bit since I had been there thirty something years before. Many of the buildings are in the U.S. National Register of Historic Places, and the city has about thirty-five hundred residents. It's the kind of town that only lists first names in the phone book because everyone knows everyone else. Come to think of it, the high school my kids attend has more people than the city of Galena. Main Street is lined with ice cream shops, adorable restaurants, specialty stores, and street vendors. I could have shopped for hours.

We walked aimlessly down Main Street and stopped in a few places, without any direction. After an hour or so of wandering, Uncle John pointed to a hillside a little way off and said, "Hey, there's Vinny Vanucchi's Restaurant. Your Aunt Pat and I went there to celebrate our wedding anniversary when we were here in June." By this time, it was close to lunch, so we decided to check it out.

We walked up the outside staircase and were offered a table on the patio of the restaurant, known to locals as "Little Italy." From its perch halfway up the hillside, we could see the traffic on the cobblestone street below and were able to witness all of the hustle and bustle going up and down Main Street. We told Uncle John all about our families and our lives. I realized that he needed us as much as we needed him to hold on to our memories of Mom. Living so far away, we had missed out on getting to know him as adults. Over the years, we had seen him at weddings and funerals, but we hadn't had the chance to connect with him in a long time. In this one weekend, we shared so much time with Uncle John that I was able to understand why he was so special to Mom. In a nutshell, he's *fun*. Seeing Uncle John doubled-over laughing at Fiona's stories was good for my soul. Laughter always heals my heart.

Uncle John drove us back to the hotel. Helen sat in the front passenger seat, and Fiona and Suson sat on both sides of me in the back. We told Uncle John about the time Shamus took his daughter to a Chinese restaurant for take-out. Shamus and his wife Kristen have five kids, and a hurricane had knocked their power out for two days so they had been eating out. The kids had practice and games on this particular night, so Shamus and Molly were just running in to order dinner and head home. They arrived at the restaurant around eight forty-five, anxious to get their food.

Shamus and his daughter went into the restaurant while the rest of the family waited in the van. The owner of the restaurant greeted them with a warm "e-woe" and asked to take their order. Shamus asked for two chicken and vegetable dinners, Kung Pao chicken, three egg rolls, three spring rolls, and two chicken and broccoli dinners. The owner of the restaurant, who was of Chinese descent, was writing everything down and asking questions about his order.

She asked, "Do you want ve-git-a-bul with chicken or just ve-git-a-bul?"

Shamus laughed and said, "Yes, chicken with vegetables."

Then she asked, "Is or-da take out or fo' here?"

Shamus said, "To go, please."

"You want doc or white meat for chicken?"

Shamus said, "It doesn't matter."

"Any dwink wis or-da?"

"Two diet cokes would be great."

She looked at her sheet, added up the total, and said, "$32.24," while ringing the register. The cashier drawer popped open with a bang, and the receipt printed out the side of the register. Just as Shamus was pulling out his debit card, he heard a loud ring. He looked up and the woman had hit the bell on the service counter. She yelled, "Sowey, we cwosed!"

Uncle John laughed and asked why the lady was so concerned with making sure his order was right.

I replied, "Because she was stalling for time. Shamus said he thought something was weird when she asked if he wanted vegetables in his chicken and vegetables."

Fiona then took the story to a new level. She made up details like the woman was looking back at the cook and making hand gestures about the order, swiping her hand in front of her neck like not to worry about it. Fiona mimicked the woman saying, "No ova-time fo' you!" She hit two fingers on her opposite wrist. "Or-da ne-va go thu."

She pretended to talk to Shamus, "You want me to cook in dis pan or da pan?" We laughed until we couldn't breathe.

When we calmed down, Uncle John sighed and said, "I wish the boys could have made this trip, too."

❈❈❈❈❈❈❈❈❈❈❈❈❈❈❈❈❈❈

We arrived back in the parking lot of the Julian Hotel and made plans for meeting up after our spa treatments. We'd be finished around five-thirty, and we would meet Uncle John in the hotel lobby. Helen and I went to start the repair on our faces and sore muscles. Suson and Fiona were heading to the room to take a nap until their appointments, and Uncle John took off for the dam to check out the birds and boats. We had been close to one another for so many hours that it felt odd to be separated. I lay on the table anxiously awaiting my facial. I knew I would be back on a plane, away from all of these people, in a matter of hours. And I had no idea when I would see them again. As wonderful as it was to be with my sisters, knowing it would end as fast as it began was always painful. I closed my eyes and thought of Fiona impersonating the Chinese lady, saying, "Or-da ne-va go thu," and I began to smile again.

When it was time for my manicure, I was still wearing my white comfy robe from my room. I browsed the nail colors before I sat down. Usually I choose clear, nothing too pretentious; but today I wanted something vivacious. I wanted a nail color that spoke to me. Something that people would notice. One particular color caught my attention. It was different, and I especially liked the name. I mean, seriously, you have to like the name of the nail color if you plan on wearing it. "Living in the Moment" had me hook, line, and sinker.

The manicurist was pleasant and asked several questions about where I was from and why I was in town. I told her I was in town with my sisters visiting my mother's grave. She kept working on a hang nail on my left hand, but she didn't talk much after that. I heard the pedicurist behind me tell her client the name of the nail polish I had used. I turned around and saw Fiona in the chair. She wanted the same polish for her toes. I said "Hi," and we laughed about having the same great taste. I thought to myself, *I wonder if that girl giving the pedicure is wearing gloves; she could catch some killer athlete's foot if she's not careful.* As my gal was handing the nail polish over, I breathed a sigh of relief that my appointment was first.

I finished up my treatments and decided to look for Uncle John. The salon was located in the lower level of the hotel, so I walked up the two flights of stairs and entered the lobby where I found hundreds of people in tuxedoes, bridesmaid dresses, and several children crying because they had obviously missed their afternoon naps. The hotel had banquet rooms, and two weddings were being held at the same time. It was total chaos, to say in the least. People were trying to check in and out, photographers were taking pictures of bridal parties on the grand stairway, and guests from both weddings looked like cows herding through the lobby. I searched for Uncle John but couldn't find him and decided to head back down to the relaxation room to wait for Helen to get ready. Walking back downstairs to the spa, I compared the lobby to my life after Mom died: It was impulsive and uncertain.

Chapter Eighteen
Flying Solo

Spring of 1986 brought new beginnings. Jimmy graduated from high school and received an engineering scholarship from Purdue University. Caroline was accepted to Miami University in Oxford, Ohio and decided to major in accounting. They had purpose, direction, and focus to succeed in college. But I didn't care about being focused, and I didn't feel like I had any purpose.

When fall arrived, I missed both of them every day. Tennis wasn't fun anymore. We had a new coach, and my treasured doubles partner wasn't there to goof off with me. The team consisted of people who took lessons all year round and only wanted to win. The record and who was going to sectionals were the only things that mattered. Surprisingly, the coach made me the team captain. I think it was because he felt sorry for me, and I had the biggest car. My 1976 Chevy station wagon got four miles to the gallon, but I could fit the whole team in it.

Dad was adjusting to his new life and role as a single father. He was home every day at five to make dinner. He made a point to go over Fiona's homework every night and was in constant contact with her teachers. He hired a cleaning lady named Sylvia who came in twice a week to do laundry, clean, and cook dinner on the nights he had to go out of town on business. He was doing his best to take care of us, and yet no one was doing anything for him. I never made an effort to help him with Fiona because I was extremely busy being defiant and depressed about my life. Mother Theresa could have walked through my front door, and I would have given her an attitude and blamed her for everything.

Although we never talked about it, I always wondered what work was like for Dad after Mom died. He was a pharmaceutical salesman, so he was constantly in and out of hospitals and doctors' offices every day of the week. Was it like throwing salt on a wound? Was it a constant reminder of the countless hours he spent with Mom trying to be positive for her?

I think after it was all said and done, he ached not only for himself, but also for Fiona, especially because she had lost so much at such a young age. The two of them became inseparable and literally saved each other from the loneliness and void they were experiencing. They went to visit Sister Pat just about every weekend. She lived and worked in a convent about three hours away in Lewis County, Kentucky, and she always had them working on a project, whether it was teaching English to the Mexicans, building a house for the homeless, or harvesting the sweet potato fields. Regardless, it kept them busy. Busy enough to feel needed, busy enough to forget, and busy enough to fall asleep every night once their heads hit their pillows. They had little time for self-pity, and their work made them appreciate the little blessings they had in their lives. Seeing how happy they could make others in need made an enormous difference in Fiona's and Dad's attitudes toward life.

The nuns treasured Fiona because she brought so much life to the convent, and she loved all the delicious meals and attention they gave her. Dad loved putting his carpentry skills to use and got a little break from being a single parent. The area was dangerous, and Fiona told me that there were bars on the windows of the convent. Dad insisted that she sleep in his room every night because he was afraid for her safety. I've always had a secret opinion that nuns are a lot tougher than they look. Maybe it has something to do with black being a power color. It always comes down to the clothes.

Caroline sent letters from school to tell me how great college life was for her. She had made new friends, was dating a guy on the swim team, and her grades were good. Deep down, I wished she wasn't so happy without me. Nonetheless, Caroline was in her element at school; she loved her new life, and I was miserable because I wasn't a part of it.

I continued working at the Hallmark store and sent letters to my Grandpa Delany on a daily basis. After over fifty years as a widower, he still lived alone. One night while I was working, he called my house just to talk to me. That was the first and last time he ever called just for me. Who knew it would take one hundred and fifty greeting cards to get a special phone call from Grandpa? Seeing the note by the phone that he had called just to talk made me feel so special.

Jimmy was only a couple of hours away, but I missed seeing him every day. He was studying chemical engineering and living the college life. He always surrounded himself with good friends that studied hard but also liked to have fun. He tried to make time for me, but I made it difficult for him. It was easier to hurt him than to deal with him hurting me. I wanted things to be the way they were, but life was constantly moving like a roller coaster, and I hated surprises. I hated the uncertainty of my fate in our relationship because I always thought he could do better than me, and I never understood what he saw in me. My senior year was isolated without my two best friends, but somehow I made it through and was accepted to Ohio State University.

The night before I left for school, I thought of Caroline as I looked around my room, my two packed suitcases waiting by my door. I was at her house the night before she left for college, and I felt like my right arm was being cut off. It was like another death to me when she left for school. Her room looked like it had been ransacked. There were boxes filled with so many new things that her dad thought they were going to have to take two cars to drop her off. Her mom had taken her out shopping and bought her a new comforter for her dorm room, new clothes, and school supplies. When it came my turn, I was in charge of my list. I grabbed twin sheets from the linen closet, and it was business as usual; I was on my own. Had I asked for something in particular, I know my Dad would have bought it for me, but I didn't know what I needed. *I just didn't know.* Helen was in England, and I didn't think to ask her or my brothers. I figured all I needed was my clothes. At seventeen, you don't have insight into the future; life is a "right now" kind of thing. The only thing I knew for certain was that the people who took an active interest in me were slowly leaving my life. Looking around my room that night, I felt my heart break.

Jimmy came to say good-bye to me that night, and I was touched and surprised by his visit. I loved him so much and part of me wanted us to stay together. I wanted us to be like we were. I wanted him to emotionally support and encourage me because he was the one person who believed in me. But I didn't want to be hurt by him. When I hugged him for the last time at my front door, I kissed him and put my face to his neck when we embraced. I smelled his Polo cologne for the last time. He was wearing a blue rugby shirt and shorts with a baseball hat. His face was rough because he hadn't shaved in a couple of days. When I decided to let go, I knew I had to release him both emotionally and physically because he represented so much of my painful past. And just like that, I never spoke to him again.

Once I got to college, I didn't sleep for four days. My world had always been so structured and strict, that I didn't know what to do with my freedom. So I did whatever I wanted. I had no sense of responsibility, and I just let myself go. That pretty much sums up my college life at OSU. I failed out twice. The first time, I didn't even tell Dad. I had failed English 101, so I had Helen write my letter of appeal. She figured she would have a better shot at it than I would. (I thought if you didn't go to class, how could they grade you? Well, they can fail you, just in case you didn't know.)

After I failed out the second time, again for not attending classes, I moved back home with my tail between my legs. I didn't know what I was going to do with myself. I worked mediocre jobs that allowed me to buy a car and pay for my car insurance while I lived at home and went to school part-time. My social life was desolate. I had no friends and about as much direction in my life as a car sliding on black ice. I dated guys from work, but I would drop them like a bad habit if I started to have feelings for them. And they weren't the marrying kind, anyway.

My family knew I was lost, but they didn't know how to help me. One day, I came to the realization that I wasn't even fit to care for myself. So, I took a five-month hiatus at Sunset Beach. My aunt Myrna lived there, and she agreed to take me under her wing if I promised to get my act together. In my time there, she taught me the true meaning of selfless love.

When I thought I was ready, I returned to Ohio. Unfortunately, I returned to some of my old ways. I tried to avoid being hurt or abandoned. I found it easier to end relationships myself than to put my fate in someone else's hands. I thought if I could control my feelings, I could keep myself from being hurt like I was when Mom died. I felt like that was the only thing I could control about my life. Well that, and my outfits.

Chapter Nineteen

The First of the Good-byes

The chaos of the lobby could have been a million miles away from downstairs. The spa was so quiet you could have heard a pin drop. I went to find Helen in the women's room, and she was blow-drying her hair. Suson was getting her massage, and I saw that Fiona was still getting her pedicure. Helen and I talked for a little bit about her services rendered before I headed back to secure a place at the bar for us. Things were still crazy in the lobby, but I saw Uncle John pacing back and forth, dodging guests and obnoxious groomsmen. I told him that I was going to wait at the bar for the other girls to finish their treatments, and he decided to join me. It was about five-forty when we walked through the doors of Julian's Restaurant. Bob's face lit up like a Christmas tree when he saw us. He immediately got Uncle John his bourbon and pulled the lever for the Guinness draft for me. You would've thought that this guy was having a party, and we were the only people who showed up for it. He didn't leave us, and he made sure the snack bowls had plenty of peanuts. The girls joined us as I finished my first beer.

Bob got Helen's cabernet, lite beer for Fiona, and a chardonnay for Suson. He made sure that everyone in our little group was happy. We hung out for a while, entertaining Bob and the wait staff as we had done the night before. Fiona told Uncle John about the day of her college graduation party when she had mistakenly taken one of Suson's hormone pills, thinking it was an Advil. She laughed as she yelled, *"What's it going to do to me?"* The place erupted.

It was almost nine o'clock when we decided that we needed to find some dinner. We said our good-byes to the staff and Bob. He made us promise that if we were ever in town again, we would come by and see him. He said that the bar hadn't seen so much excitement and life in years, and we would be missed. I think our bill was probably more than Bob had seen in months.

We left the Julian Hotel and walked down Harper Street looking for something delicious. Helen noticed a pizza sign, and we ran towards it like vultures. Our sensational lunch was long gone, and we were starving. We found a little booth in the back of the restaurant and piled in. After we ordered our pizza, we noticed that Uncle John got a little quiet. Something was different about him.

When the pizza arrived, you would have thought that none of us had never seen food before. I'm not sure if it was the recipe or the fact that I was ravenous, but it was the best pizza I had ever eaten in my entire life. Uncle John insisted on paying our bill, and we all staggered out of the place.

Uncle John needed to leave by ten, and we only had a few minutes left with him. He looked at his watch as we ambled back to the hotel. The entire mood had changed drastically. No one knew what to say. I have never handled this part of the trip very well because I *hate* saying good-bye. I hadn't seen our precious uncle in eight years, and I couldn't help thinking another eight years would go by before we saw each other again. I didn't want this weekend to end. We had shared so much that it didn't seem right for him to just get in the car and drive off. None of us wanted him to go.

We walked him to his car, and he gave each of us a piece of bubble gum. He joked that our breath was bad and chuckled. He gave out hugs and kissed us each on the cheek. When it came to my turn to say good-bye to him, I didn't want to let go. He was the closest thing I had to my mom, and for the first time that I could remember, I felt like she was with us. I saw Mom in his laugh, when he smiled, and when he talked about Grandpa Delany. When I finally let go of him I said, "I love you,

Uncle John. Thank you so much for coming. We couldn't have done what we did today if you hadn't been here to help us."

He replied, "I'm glad I could be with you guys. You made your Mom proud by coming out here."

And with those last words, he got into his car and drove out of the parking lot. Fiona and Suson pulled out their cigarettes and lighters and smoked a couple outside of the hotel. I pretended like I was taking one for the team and smoked one, too. I hated that I enjoyed it as much as I did. Our group didn't feel complete without Uncle John. Helen insisted that we try a different bar in the hotel because it wouldn't be the same if we went to visit Bob again without Uncle John. The bar on the second floor had a cozy outside seating area, and the four of us settled in with our drinks to talk about the day.

Chapter Twenty
Where Did It Go?

I woke up the next morning to a lingering stale smell, which I discovered was Suson's bad breath, and a throbbing headache. I pushed the covers back and swung my legs over the side of the bed very slowly. Headache or no headache, I wasn't about to walk anywhere without shoes on my feet. Both panels of the drapes were closed, and the room was as black as night. I fumbled for my shoes, searching for them with my toes. I found one flip flop and then the other. I walked around the bed and grabbed my purse on the desk. I knew I had a bottle of Tylenol in there somewhere. I held my purse with my left hand and felt with my right hand aimlessly for the bottle. I found it and walked to the bathroom to get a cup of water.

When I turned on the light, it blinded me, and I cursed out loud. I tried to close the door quickly, so I wouldn't wake the girls, but Helen was already at the door telling me she had to use the bathroom. Apparently, I wasn't as quiet as I thought I was because everyone was awake. Fiona was out of bed and looking for her phone again, and Suson was pulling back the drapes to let some light in the room. The clock read seven twenty-five in bright red numbers. We had gone to bed around two-thirty, so it was no wonder I was exhausted. I sat down on the bed with my water and Tylenol in hand and took everything in. There were empty water bottles on the night stand, The Collection was everywhere but the closet, and we all looked completely drained from our lack of sleep during the last seventy-two hours. There wasn't enough makeup in a Revlon factory to make any of us look slightly better. Everything from the weekend came flooding back to me. So much had happened. The still frame pictures in my mind were vibrant, and I hoped they would stay that way. Most importantly, I felt at peace...I was able to let go of my guilt over my mother's death with Helen and Fiona by my side.

We packed up the room and headed to breakfast at Julian's Restaurant, a.k.a. Bob's Place, where we were seated in a booth. The waiter was cute and had more of a Southern accent than a country singer singing at a pig pickin'. He became a Chatty Kathy when I told him I was from South Carolina. I could hear Fiona's stomach growling, but I didn't know how to make him go away. He really was a nice kid, but I'm not sure how a Southern boy ended up land-locked in Dubuque, Iowa. I didn't ask because I wanted to eat my breakfast once it arrived. I was pretty hungry, too. Even though Bob was a talker, he still got his work done. This guy obviously wasn't trained by Bob.

We paid for breakfast and went back upstairs to gather our things in the room. We made sure that we didn't leave anything behind. I was especially concerned about The Collection, since it had been all over the room earlier that morning. We headed down the elevator to the first floor, and I checked us out of the hotel, while the girls walked to the parking lot and waited for me. When I signed my name on the bill, I had that feeling again that it was over. Part of me was sad, but the other part was ready to get home and see my family. I really missed them. That's another great thing about these weekends, as much fun as I have with my sisters, the time away always makes me appreciate Tom and my kids when I get back.

When I put my luggage in the back of Fiona's car, I could tell the mood had changed. Everyone was silent and melancholy. We drove out of the parking lot, and it felt like we were leaving something behind. The radio was playing some tune, and all of us but Fiona had our heads turned, looking out our side windows, deep in thought. Maybe we were all processing. It reminded me of the silence after Mom died. No one said what she really thought or felt; we just acted like nothing had happened. Like the first day back at school after Mom had died over Christmas break.

❊❊❊❊❊❊❊❊❊❊❊❊❊❊❊❊❊❊

In high school, we had A-day and B-day schedules. I hated A-days because I never saw Jimmy or Caroline. My first day back was an A-day. People noticed me and knew what had happened to my mom, but they didn't talk to me at all. I guess they didn't know what to say. You would expect it from kids my age, but not my teachers. All day long, the only thing I heard when I walked down the hallway towards my locker was, "That's the sweater she wore to the funeral."

I wanted to scream at the top of my lungs, "Why wouldn't I wear it?" It was the only gift I got for Christmas besides the sporting equipment; Jimmy had given it to me. It was a black cardigan with silver buttons and two thin vertical stripes—one red and one white—down the front of the sweater. It matched my red wool skirt perfectly, and I wore it with my white lace tights and black flats. I loved that outfit. When everything else was amiss, I knew I could always find comfort in my clothes. I believed if I looked good on the outside, no one would be able to tell how I was feeling on the inside.

I didn't have a session with the guidance counselor that day or a talk with the principal about my feelings. No one said anything to me about my mom. I wanted desperately for someone to say *something* about the funeral or about what had happened, but no one did. It was the longest day of my life. I could feel stares and hear people talking about me. The problem was, no one was talking *to* me.

❊❊❊❊❊❊❊❊❊❊❊❊❊❊❊❊❊❊

Three almost-completely-silent hours later, we arrived in Chicago at O'Hare to drop Helen and Suson off to catch their flights. We gave each other hugs and said our good-byes, but it was quick with no emotion. *Why, I wonder, is it that Helen and Fiona are good at good-byes and I'm not? Why can't I be strong like they are?*

After we left them, Fiona and I hunkered down for the rest of the drive to Dayton. We had five more hours to go, and we were beat.

We didn't talk much, but we listened to her Joni Mitchell CD, and all I wanted to do was cry. I realized it wasn't grief or guilt; it was simply the feeling of being alone—without my sisters, Suson, and Uncle John. I didn't want the closeness that I felt with them to end.

Fiona got a phone call from Sterling, who had been playing golf with his boss. He decided to meet us for dinner in Dayton around six. Fiona picked some Mexican restaurant. We pulled into the parking lot around six-fifteen, and I was proud of myself for making it through the drive without breaking down. The hardest part was over.

We walked into the restaurant, and Sterling stood up from a table to let us know where he was seated. He gave us hugs and kisses and offered us what was left of his chips. He had eaten most of the basket since he had been waiting for us for twenty minutes. The waitress came, and we ordered while Sterling asked us about the weekend. Fiona told him about 1722 Van Buren and the letter we read from Dad to the Henschkes. She told him about how much fun we had with Uncle John and how Uncle Dick promised us autographed posters of Kurt Warner and him. He told her about his golf game, and our food arrived. I was quiet until Sterling asked me a question. I suddenly began to cry. I cried and I cried. I tried to stop, but there was no use. I didn't want to eat, and I didn't finish my drink. I could tell that Fiona wasn't upset about me crying, but she didn't know how to deal with me either. She can usually say something to snap me out of my fits, but nothing worked.

We paid our bill, got back into the car, and headed to Fiona and Sterling's house to spend the night. My flight home wasn't until the next afternoon. I tried to shake it off by the time we made it back to their place. I tried to apologize, but it just made me cry more. I couldn't even finish a sentence. I have cried a lot in my life, but this episode was complete insanity.

The next morning I awoke to my eyes swollen shut. I managed to open them just enough to look in the mirror. My reflection reminded me of a horror show. I seriously thought I was going to have trouble boarding my flight home being that I didn't look like my photo at all. My whole face was distorted. I walked into the kitchen where Fiona was brewing coffee, and she couldn't help but laugh. She pulled out ice cubes and put them in a Ziploc bag, so I could put them on my eyes. We walked out to the back patio. She carried the coffee, and I carried the ice. We sat down and the hot sun felt wonderful on my face. I apologized for my behavior the night before. "I don't know what came over me, Fiona, but I don't think I have ever cried that hard in my entire life. I'm so embarrassed and feel like such an idiot. I'm sorry I ruined our last night."

Fiona took a sip of her coffee, put it back on the table, picked up a cigarette, and lit it. She exhaled the smoke and said, "I get it. When I came back from visiting Uncle John last summer, I did the same thing. Remember cousin Annie's wedding last summer was in Milwaukee? Y'all couldn't come because Seth had All-Stars. Well, Sterling and I drove to Madison and had dinner with Uncle John and Aunt Pat. Dinner was great, and then we went back to their house and sat up until like two in the morning. We had a blast. But then, Sterling and I sat at this very same table when we got back in town, and I was a mess. You should have seen me. I totally get it. It's great to see him, but it's tough, too, because he was so close to Mom. It's okay, Megan, but your face is a disaster." We both laughed.

She dropped me off at Dad's house just after ten, so I could spend time with him before I left for the airport. He met us in the driveway, spoke with Fiona for a little, and then we said our good-byes. She gave me a hug and said, "Call me when you get home."

"I will," I replied as I hugged her back.

She got in her car, backed out of the driveway, and drove down the street.

I had a couple of hours before my flight, and I talked my dad's ears off. I told him about the windmills in Indiana, walking through 1722 Van Buren, St. Stephen's School, and all the things I remembered about our old house. I told him about being at Mom's grave, spending the day in Galena, and learning so many things about Uncle John. We had a really good talk about Mom and how proud she would be that Helen, Fiona, and I make time for each other year. I realized later that I didn't cry at all during our visit. I was surprised. Fiona said it was because I was dehydrated. She's a smartass, but she was probably right.

When my flight landed in Charleston, I was so excited to see Tom that I had forgotten I put my purse under my seat on the plane. I walked through security and went to pull out my lip balm but didn't have it. Security wouldn't let me go back to the plane, so I had to wait until someone from US AIR could retrieve it for me. So while I was sitting there in the baggage claim, exhausted with swollen eyes, I thought of how this could have been my life had things gone differently. *That lady retrieving my purse could have been me working for an airline,* I thought to myself.

My flight attendant training in St. Louis, Missouri, seemed like a lifetime ago. I was young and ready to travel the world. It was a completely different life path; nonetheless, it led me to my husband and three beautiful children. I wondered whatever happened to Ted. *If I ran into him, would he remember me? And why do I still shove everything into my suitcase haphazardly when I was taught how to properly pack a suitcase?*

Chapter Twenty-One
The Island of Misfits

B ack in the spring of 1990, five years after Mom died, I was skipping class, which I did frequently in college while living at home. I read an advertisement in the classifieds that interviews were being held in Cincinnati, Ohio, for flight attendants. I thought about it, grabbed my purse from the counter, and headed to J. C. Penny's to buy a new outfit for my interview. I had found my direction: I was going to travel the world.

I talked with Dad, and he said I should go for it. He even gave me gas money for the hour drive to the interview. When I arrived at the hotel where the interviews for Trans World Airlines were being held, I thought I was at a model scouting because every person was about six feet tall and gorgeous. I pulled my briefcase closer to my chest. I felt more confident and secure the tighter I held it to my body. Everyone around me looked beautiful and smart, exactly how a flight attendant was supposed to look. I questioned the woman at the table about where I was to go because people were filling out forms, stepping on scales, and being called into the back room.

"Do you have a résumé?" The woman asked, without even looking at me.

I cleared my throat, "Yes." I had to clear my throat again since I had been in the car for over an hour and hadn't talked to anyone. "Yes," I said and smiled the best I could, so she could see I was perfect flight attendant material. You know, friendly with people.

"Okay, fill out this form and sit in the area to your left. Someone will call you back. There will be three different people talking to you today, so plan on being here for a couple of hours."

"Thanks," I said and smiled really big before I walked over to my left, only to find no seat available. So, I found a spot in the corner and started filling out the form. One of the questions was: *Do you get headaches?* I looked to the person on my right, trying to make a new friend, and said, "Yeah, question twelve about getting headaches? Um, I just get those when I fly. Do you think they will frown upon that?" I laughed, but my potential new friend did not. I decided not to try and make any more friends.

They called my name, and I headed to the back room smiling from ear to ear and making eye contact with everyone I passed. Someone was going to see what a people person I was if it killed me. Ironically, my smiling was wasted on an interviewer who didn't ask any questions, but put me on a scale to make sure that my height and weight were in proportion. Considering I was about twenty pounds *under* the expected weight for my height, I was automatically pushed to the next level of interviews. The next interviewer asked me about my family, and I told her that my mother had died from cancer five years before. She looked me in the eye, put her pen down very tenderly, and said, "Mine too."

It was the first time I had met someone who had been through the same thing I had. Her name was Janine and her mother had died when she was eighteen from cancer. She told me a little about her mother's disease and progression, and I hoped she would give me advice or help me find closure. I asked her how she dealt with her pain and if it ever got easier. She very casually picked her pen back up and said, "You just get over it. Everything changes with time. Okay let's talk about career goals."

Janine must have felt sorry for me because I was selected for the third interview. The interview was a group interview with five other applicants in front of a panel of three Trans World flight attendants. They drilled us with questions about typical problems on a plane and how we would handle them. I guess I answered everything well enough, or maybe it was my dazzling smile, because I was chosen for a final interview in St. Louis, Missouri.

I flew to the interview in St. Louis, did well, and was offered a position for the upcoming flight attendant training session that was being held there. Training lasted for seven weeks with an assignment in New York working out of JFK airport flying international flights upon successful completion. I shared a hotel room with three other girls who were more confused and lost than even I was at that point in my life. I knew why I was there: I was a drifter with no direction who desperately needed her mother's guidance, I was qualified to do nothing, and I wanted to find happiness again. I wanted to escape from my life because I knew I was emotionally broken. Jimmy had graduated college and was dating someone seriously. Caroline was an accountant at a successful firm in downtown Dayton with a new boyfriend, and I was nothing. The day I arrived at my temporary home in St. Louis, I knew I had officially landed on the Island of Misfits.

All three of my roommates were from the east coast and had unique personalities. Allison was eighteen years old from Hoboken, New Jersey, and didn't have a dime to her name. She unpacked fourteen cartons of cigarettes from her suitcase along with three different outfits, which she promptly hung in the closet. She also removed and hung up the one she was originally wearing when we met an hour before we were given our room assignments. At first I thought she was changing her clothes, but when she didn't change into anything, I started to feel uncomfortable. She informed us that she didn't like to be confined to clothes when she was resting, which happened to be any time she was in our room.

Lydia was from New York City and had never held a job in her life. She was extremely sheltered and privileged and this job was all about cutting the cord from "Daddy." Her father was drinking buddies with Carl Icahn who happened to be the Chief Executive Officer of TWA at the time. She oozed money when she walked into the room with her matching Chanel luggage and Gucci purse.

Susan was from Charlotte, North Carolina, and had failed the bar exam three times. She always had her nose in a book, particularly her old law textbooks, and she had obviously taken this job to pay her rent in the hopes of eventually passing the test. She objected to literally *any* type of humor. She was almost as much fun as a migraine.

We had extensive training for each plane: 727, 747, and the L1011, which included lessons in hijacking procedures, bar cart service, protecting the cockpit at all costs, and exceptional customer service. The first week weeded out a few people because it showed the non-glamorous side of a flight attendant's job. Hijacking and fires aboard the plane were very realistic scenarios, and I had to close my eyes a few times because I didn't want to think about something so horrific ever happening when I was working. We watched plane after plane blown into tiny pieces and too many terrorists with black masks and AK-47 assault rifles. At times it was a bit overwhelming, but I just tried to think about the positives: shopping in Paris, a really cool suitcase with wheels, and designer brand uniforms. Ralph Lauren designed the uniforms for TWA, and wearing Ralph Lauren every day was a dream come true. With that wardrobe, I wasn't losing this job for anything.

We started with thirty-two people in my class, all between the ages of eighteen and fifty. I became good friends with a girl from Beaufort, South Carolina, named Mary Hunt Jenkins. I met her in the hallway outside our rooms at the hotel one night. I wanted to use the pay phone, and she was talking to her boyfriend. She had just found out that he had another girlfriend, and she was *not* happy about it. Even though I tried not to listen, I couldn't help but overhear their conversation.

"John, you can keep your trailer trash girlfriend because you'll never be worthy of *me!*" She hung up the phone and wiped her eyes. When she looked up, she noticed me and walked over to introduce herself. She had beautiful long, curly blonde hair with just the perfect amount of pink in her cheeks and the sweetest southern accent I'd ever heard. She made everything sound interesting and inviting. "Well, hey there. My name is Mary Hunt Jenkins, but you can call me MJ."

I shook her hand and realized she was my lifeline off the Island of Misfits. MJ had a great sense of humor, her daddy's credit card, and impeccable style. We talked for three hours that night in the hallway bonding over our mutual love for shopping and discussing our dreams and plans.

MJ lived by three rules. She always stressed that a woman should be treated like a lady, carry perfume and lipstick in her purse at all times, and always salt and butter her grits. She believed that one should nourish the soul with good people, that money *could*, in fact, buy happiness, and that grits were acceptable for any meal. She was everything I wanted to be: free, self-aware, independent (well, sort of, if we didn't count her dad's credit card), and confident in all of her decisions. I envied her ability to be carefree when I was so far from that. However, one thing was certain: MJ was fun to be around, and I really needed some fun in my life.

One day in class, we were studying procedures for crash landings. The instructor asked us what steps we should take before impact. He paced back and forth in front of the classroom, trying to make an impact on us. "Ladies and gentlemen we have five minutes before a crash landing, the ground has been notified, and the pilots have rung the four bells throughout the cabin. What needs to be done to the cabin and galley? What do we need to do to prepare for the landing?"

Possible answers included securing the galley, reassuring the passengers, and making sure cabinets were fastened and overhead compartments were securely closed. MJ looked at me and smiled big before raising her hand. I knew whatever she was going to say was going to be good. The instructor called on MJ, and she said in her best Southern accent, "Freshen up my lipstick, you know, for the TV cameras that will be filming our evacuation from the plane."

The instructor's mouth dropped to the floor and the room erupted into laughter. It was just another day in class with MJ.

Two weeks later, we had to study for our bar exam, which consisted of preparing different types of drinks and garnishes that we would serve on the plane. MJ decided that we needed to go to happy hour and "live the experience." She said, "We have an assimilator for fire and smoke appears; we have people that are masked and pretend to be terrorists; we use the bar cart and practice going up and down the aisles...this is the same thing."

It made sense to me. My roommates wanted nothing to do with us since we were drinking on a school night. They scolded us for leaving, but that didn't stop us. MJ called a taxi, and we headed to a bar that was a known hangout for instructors at the academy. We ordered drinks and quizzed the bartender on garnishes. We saw two of our safety instructors, Ted and John, and hung out with them. Four hours later, with MJ's daddy's credit card, we were ready for the test.

We aced the bar test the next day with flying colors, along with all the other safety and service tests we took over the next couple of weeks, gaining a little respect from our classmates. Although we should have been celebrating our great grades, the Persian Gulf War was in full swing, and it was all over the news. People at the TWA Academy were getting pink slips like invitations to a Sweet Sixteen birthday party. Instructors were leaving in the middle of lectures, yet no one told us what was really happening. The new instructors that took over our classes assured us that we didn't need to worry. Nevertheless, my unsocial roommate Susan was reading *10 Things You Need To Know To Pass the Bar Exam* and the *Kaplan Bar Review* during class. Allison went from one pack a day to two from the stress, and Lydia was constantly on the pay phone trying to find her dad to see if he knew anything about our demise. Ironically, he was usually drinking at a bar somewhere and wasn't able to help us.

I knew I wanted to be a flight attendant more than anything, but what bothered me most was that I felt like I was finally in the right place with the right people, and I was afraid it was going to end. I had direction and purpose, and I was really good at what I was doing and it showed. I felt important carrying my Flight Service Manual to class and wearing my TWA badge. I knew I was really happy because I wasn't worried about which outfit I would wear to class every day. For the first time I could remember, I wasn't hiding behind my clothes. It was a good feeling.

Chapter Twenty-Two
Back to Square One

Two days before our graduation from flight attendant training, we were notified of a terrorist attack that killed eight crew members aboard an international flight to Dublin, Ireland. Classes were dismissed at three that afternoon, and everyone headed to the bar where MJ and I studied for our bar exam. All of the instructors from the Academy were there, as well as the pilots that were being trained for TWA and their instructors. The mood was especially somber because three of the crew members had graduated from the Academy less than six months before. When we walked in, we noticed our buddies at the bar. MJ and I walked over to Ted and John. They told us that they were friends with the male pilots, and they had trained the female flight attendant only a couple of months before. Ted specifically remembered the girl because she had almost quit during the first week. She couldn't handle watching the terrorist attacks. He told us that he was the one who had convinced her to stay. He couldn't finish the rest of his sentence because he was so upset. That's when it became real to me. Real in the sense that I could die or see someone else killed. I started to have my doubts. *Is this the life for me? Is it worth the cool uniforms and the rolling suitcase? Will I even make enough money to buy cool things in Paris? Do I even know how much money I will be making a year? Crap! I don't have a clue how much money I'm going to make, and MJ said we have to buy our uniforms. Well there's nothing I can do about it now,* I thought to myself as I ordered another drink.

Four hours later, we professed our undying friendship with everyone in the bar and exchanged numbers and addresses, so we could stay in touch with our soon-to-be fellow co-workers.

When the bus picked us up at the hotel the next morning, my head was pounding from my outrageous hangover. I was wearing my sunglasses and didn't notice that four people were still M.I.A. from the night before. We had two classes scheduled that day, and both dealt with how to pack a suitcase. I was so exhausted that I literally thought about putting toothpicks in my eyes to keep them open. I wasn't wearing any makeup because I overslept. Class was manageable, but I was counting down the hours until I could go back to the hotel and sleep. After class, I ran into Ted and John, and they looked worse than I did. Ted told me that he needed to talk to me and asked if I would meet him later that evening. We agreed to meet outside the hotel near the rear entrance since fraternizing with the students was not allowed. He would pick me up there. I agreed but was a little concerned about his demeanor. He seemed very sad and serious.

When I told MJ what I was doing, she insisted that I take her dad's credit card in case I had an emergency, and she wouldn't take no for an answer. She also made me change my outfit because I "wasn't wearing my colors." She insisted I wear a cute dress, cowboy boots, and borrow her purse for the evening along with her lipstick since I didn't own any.

Ted was out back waiting for me in his 1969 red Ford convertible Mustang when I got there, and he complimented me on how pretty I looked.

"I just threw this old thing on," I said as I tried to change the subject. "I was really worried about you today. Are you okay? I can't imagine how you must be feeling about everything. If you want to talk about anything, I'm a really good listener. Just for the record, I was a psychology major for two weeks in college," I said nervously as I strapped on my seat belt, smiling as we drove out of the parking lot.

He turned onto the main road and said, "That's good to know. I just want to have a chance to get to know you before you leave.

I want to know what makes you laugh, your likes and dislikes, and if you're dating anybody?"

I looked at him and laughed, "Oooooh, so that's what this is all about."

"Megan, I have been waiting six weeks to ask you out because as an instructor, I could lose my job. I've been working at the academy for four years and have met hundreds of women, and you are the only one I have ever asked out. I think you're funny and smart and beautiful...especially when you smile." He looked at me and winked. "The first time I saw you, I knew you were special. I just want to know if there is a possibility of you ever dating somebody like me? I'm usually not this forward, but since you're leaving in two days, I had to take a chance and tell you or I'd regret it for the rest of my life."

I sat in the passenger's side and tried to give him a serious look. "You know about my roommate Allison, don't you?" I tried not to laugh. We had talked at length about Allison's nudity the night before at the bar and how it was driving all of us in the room crazy. I had told him that two guys from the pilot training has asked me out, so they could go back to my room and see Allison.

He laughed and said, "Everybody knows about Allison, but she has nothing to do with you. So about my question...?"

"Well, we might be able to work something out."

"Okay, that's the first time I've ever heard *that* answer," he chuckled.

"Ted, I can assure you that if we do date, you will have your hands full with me." He didn't have a clue what a mess I was. *But*, I thought to myself, *who am I to tell him?*

"I think I like the sound of that. I'm going to take that as a yes for now, and I'm starving. How about you?"

"I haven't eaten anything since breakfast, and right now, I'm more into quantity than quality."

Ted laughed and replied, "Megan, you're my kind of girl."

We went to the hill and ate at Dominic's Little Italian Restaurant. We had a great time. We talked about our families, college, pilot training, and how he ended up at the Academy. Thirteen hours later, we headed back to my hotel. We had been out all night and hadn't stopped talking. Sleep was never an option since we knew our time was coming to an end. When he dropped me off, I turned to him to say good-bye, and he reached up and pulled my face towards him. He kissed me so tenderly that it sent shivers down my spine. I opened my eyes, and he said to me, "I will love you forever if you give me the chance."

I walked back to my room and tried to process everything that had happened. I couldn't deny that Ted was an amazing guy. MJ was in the hallway when I got up to my room. She looked me in the eye and teased, "I think *somebody* is smitten with Instructor Ted."

The next twenty-four hours were busy as we prepared for our move. MJ and I planned for hours in the hallway as we made the final preparations for our apartment in Hoboken, New Jersey. As much as Allison drove us crazy, she was the hook up on cheap apartments because her mother worked for a slumlord in the Jersey area. It was the perfect location because it was close enough to the airport, but far enough away from the big prices of New York City that we needed to avoid. We had planned for six of us girls working for TWA to share a two-bedroom apartment. The only bad news was that Allison was one of the six. MJ promised me that Allison would not be in our room, so it was an easy decision.

After our graduation ceremony, we all headed to our now-favorite drinking establishment. MJ had hired a limo to drive us to the bar, so we could immediately start our celebration. Several of us had less than twenty-four hours before our first flight to San Juan, Puerto Rico. We were truly excited about our new lives and future adventures. Lydia was buying drinks for everyone, and Allison was bumming cigarettes off anyone she could find. She was also telling everyone how hot it was in the bar and questioning whether or not the air conditioning was working.

John and Ted were at the graduation, but I didn't see them afterwards because we left so quickly. MJ spotted Ted at the bar and motioned to me that he was headed my way. When I turned to look in his direction, he was already there and planted a big wet kiss on my lips.

"Way to go! You had the highest GPA in the last eight classes. I wanted to congratulate you personally."

"Um, is this how they, I mean TWA, tells everyone?" I said, still a little shell-shocked that he kissed me in front of everybody in the bar.

"Only the special ones," he replied as he looked me in the eye and smiled. "Can I buy you a drink?"

"I'm thinking more like a chili dog. I'm starving and would love some alone time with you before I leave in the morning…."

"That sounds good to me. I know the perfect place," he said as he took my hand and guided me through the bar.

We hopped into his mustang and drove to Audi-K's, a drive-in known for their delicious hotdogs. We had the best chili dogs I had ever eaten in my entire life. We talked and talked and talked about life, family, and dreams. Before I knew it, the sun was coming up and I had to head back. My flight home was leaving in less than two hours. I still hadn't packed and had a lot to do. Ted dropped me off and offered to help me, but I insisted that I was fine and would call him later when I was ready to go to the airport. When I arrived upstairs, Allison had already left, Lydia was waiting for a taxi, and Susan was sitting at her desk reading her *Kaplan Bar Review* book.

"Hey, guys. What's up?" No one said anything to me. I thought it was kind of odd, but I just started putting my things together. Everyone was unusually quiet, but I didn't pay much attention. I just kept packing as fast as I could. I went to the closet and pulled out my dresses and skirts and then threw my shoes in haphazardly before starting on the dresser drawers. I used none of the new skills I had been taught; I was in too much of a hurry. MJ walked into the room. Her eyes where swollen, and she had obviously been crying.

"MJ, what's the matter?"

"We're going home, Megan."

"I know that. That's why I'm packing. My flight leaves in like two hours."

"Megan, TWA is furloughing two thousand employees. Carl Icahn is in bankruptcy and filing Chapter Eleven. Lydia was on the phone with her dad all night. Apparently, he told her to walk away now because if we were to fly overseas, we could be stuck there without pay, with no way of getting home, and at the mercy of another airline."

I sat on the floor next to my suitcase and looked at the ground. I didn't want to make eye contact with anyone because my mind was racing. I heard Susan and MJ talking, but I was tuning them out. I didn't want to hear what they had to say because I knew they were all going back to something when they went home. Lydia's dad would find her another job, and her mother would be thrilled she was coming back. MJ's dad had already made arrangements for her to have an apartment and told her to take her time getting a job. Even Susan would eventually become an attorney. But me? I was going home to nothing.

"Megan. Megan?" MJ bent down and sat next to me on the floor and put her arm on my shoulder. "Hey, it's going to be okay. I promise that you and I are going to keep in touch, and all of this is going to blow over in a couple of months. I saw John, and he told me that they will call us back when all of this is over. It just really sucks right now, but we're going to be okay." She paused for a moment, reached for a tissue, and handed it to me. "You want to share a ride to the airport?"

I thought about it before I answered. I knew I was supposed to call Ted, but my heart wasn't in it. Everything had changed in my mind. *He's too good for me, and I was crazy to think this would work,* I thought.

"Yeah, let me hop in the shower. I can be ready in about twenty minutes, okay?"

"My cab's here! I'm leaving, guys," Lydia called out. "If you're ever in New York give me a call, and I would love to do lunch."

She gave us hugs and walked out the door, knowing we would never see each other again.

Twenty-five minutes later, MJ walked down to my room and informed me that our cab was waiting for us downstairs. She helped me with my bags, and we said good-bye to Susan, who barely looked up at us to acknowledge our departure. I threw my last bag in the trunk, hopped in the back of the cab, and closed the door. At that moment, I realized my leaving symbolized my relationship with Ted. I was going to close the door on that, too. I wouldn't have airline benefits to fly back and forth for free.

I looked down and noticed that my pants didn't match my top, and my shoes weren't the right brown for my outfit. I was going to have to change my clothes in the bathroom once I got to the airport. I couldn't be seen like that in public. Everyone would see right through me.

Chapter Twenty-Three
Mint Tulips

Dad and Fiona met me at the baggage claim back in Dayton. My dad walked over to me and said, "I'm proud of you, Megan." Apparently, TWA was all over the news, so they knew about everything before I arrived.

I smirked and said, "Thanks, Dad. Not only did I graduate from flight attendant training, but I also got my pink slip. I have nothing to show for the last seven weeks. How can you be 'proud?'"

He put both of his hands on my shoulders and said, "You took a chance, Megan, and it didn't work out. I'm proud of you for trying. I know firsthand how difficult it is to try so hard at something and then fail. But I know for a fact it makes you stronger. Failure is a part of life, Megan. You're going to be okay." I started crying uncontrollably, and he pulled me closer to him.

Within two weeks, I had a job waitressing and was enrolled back in school, determined to take a full load of courses and not drop any of them. I spoke with MJ on the phone about once a week, and she always made me laugh about our lives. Her father had taken her to a psychologist to take a personality and aptitude test. He felt bad about TWA and wanted to give MJ some guidance. The test concluded that she would be very successful as a mortician.

"Okay, I'm such a people person that I need to be with dead people? That test was totally inadequate and ridiculous. I'm upset that Daddy didn't just give me the four hundred dollars. I would have found direction at TJ Maxx," she joked.

Between work and school, I had little time to think about how sad I was that things didn't work out with TWA. Helen came home for a couple of weeks, and I enjoyed spending some much-needed time with her. She and her husband loved Windsor, England, and she didn't think they'd be back in the states permanently for years. Fiona was away at college, loving life and pursuing a degree in communications with an internship set up in Washington, DC, for the spring. Things seemed to be working out for everyone but me. I felt like I was a gerbil in a tiny box running on a wheel going nowhere fast.

I had been home for about eight months when MJ called to inform me that she had convinced her father to buy me a plane ticket for her birthday. He had agreed, so I was going to fly down there for a couple days and stay at her apartment. She told me not to worry about spending money because that was included in the birthday present. I was so excited, and she already the whole weekend planned from beginning to end. I knew we were going to have a blast.

Dad drove me to the airport and said he'd pick me up Sunday night at the same place when I got back into town. As I grabbed my bag from the back seat, he asked, "Do you have your wallet?"

"Yep, I have it, and a couple of bucks, too," I grinned as I threw my bag over my shoulder.

He smiled, handed me a twenty, and said, "Lunch is on me. Have fun."

"Thanks, Dad," I said, closing the car door.

When I walked inside the airport, I was informed of Tropical Storm Bernie and that my flight was going to be re-routed to Charlotte, North Carolina, with a three-hour layover. *Perfect,* I thought. *I might as well buy some magazines, so I have something to read.* I used the twenty Dad had given me, bought three magazines, and boarded the plane. The flight to Charlotte was about an hour, and we landed in Terminal C of the airport. I grabbed my bag and found the nearest bar. I had three hours to kill. Only two seats remained, so I chose the closest one. The airport was unusually crowed because of the storm.

Men were on either side of me when I sat down. They sat up a little straighter and tried to clean up their messes. One guy had his newspaper spread out, and the other was eating his lunch with his utensils and napkins all over the bar. Once they cleared a spot for me, I ordered a beer and pulled out my magazines to check the new fall fashion colors. I minded my own business, enjoying the time alone and my beer. The guy who was eating on my right asked me if I wanted a french fry. I looked at him, not sure how to respond, and said, "No, thanks. I'm fine."

He gave me a bizarre laugh, almost like the character in the movie *The Shining*, and said, "You skinny bitches are all the same. You never want to eat."

I tried to be polite, but he was starting to scare me. So I lied through my teeth and said, "I just took medication, and I can't eat anything for two hours. I appreciate the offer, though."

He looked at me and said, "Lady, you just took medication, and you can't eat, but you're drinking a beer? That doesn't make sense." He looked disgusted.

"Okay, fine. Would you buy that I'm fasting for world hunger, but I'm allowed to drink liquid? I'm really hungry, but the beer fills me up."

The bartender cracked a smile. All I wanted was to read my stupid magazines, but this guy was badgering me to eat a soggy french fry for no good reason.

"Sorry for bothering you." He flipped some bills and change on the counter, grabbed his jacket, and stomped out of the bar.

The patrons sitting at the bar started clapping. Apparently he had been bothering a lot of people, not just me. The bartender told me that anything I wanted was on the house. I smiled with delight and ordered the Galactic Dog with chili, cheddar cheese, coleslaw, and spicy mustard. My dog came, and I enjoyed every last bit. I discovered that orange was the new color for fall and drank another beer. I thought that Charlotte must be an edgy place because a lot of people were wearing the color orange; however, come to find out, it was because of nearby Clemson University. I glanced at my watch and saw that I had less than an hour to go before my flight left for Beaufort. I asked the bartender to watch my stuff while I went to the ladies' room. When I came back, there was a good-looking guy about my age sitting in the chair next to mine. I pulled my chair out and said, "Hi."

He smiled, returned the greeting, and mentioned the ball game that was on television. He was chatty, but I didn't mind. I fell hard and fast for his Southern accent. Plus, I just wanted to stare at him all day.

"Can I buy you a drink? You look like you could use a refill." He smiled and motioned for the bartender.

"That would be great, thanks. What's your name, by the way?"

"Ha. Where are my manners? It's Tom. Tom Moller. It's a pleasure to meet you."

I put my hand out to shake his and said, "The pleasure is all mine. I'm Megan O'Malley."

"Ms. O'Malley, where are you traveling today?" He signaled the bartender with two fingers to let him know that we needed two more beers.

"I'm going to see a dear friend of mine in Beaufort, South Carolina. I guess you could say we used to work together, and I haven't seen her in about nine months. She has the whole weekend planned, and I'm really excited about it."

"I'm familiar with that area. It's a beautiful city," he said as he took a sip of his beer.

"I know nothing about it. All I know is that MJ is picking me up from the airport. What's it like?"

"It's a quaint coastal town. The downtown has a great night life, with good bands and restaurants, and everybody knows everybody—or at least that's what I've heard."

"Perfect. So you're saying that if we run into people tonight who annoy us, we're probably going to run into them all weekend."

He laughed and said, "Well, that's one way to look at it, but maybe the people you meet will be fun to be around. You might even *enjoy* running into them again?"

"I'm not usually that lucky," I said. "You should have seen the tool that was just sitting in your seat before you arrived."

"Oh, yeah?"

"You know what? He's not worth wasting my breath. Are you coming or going today?"

"I'm going home."

I wanted to ask him where home was, but I heard my boarding call over the loudspeaker.

"That's my flight. I better get going. It was really nice to meet you. Thanks for hanging out and for the beer. I hope you have a safe trip home, wherever it is."

"You too, Megan. I hope you don't run into too many people who annoy you when you're in Beaufort."

I smiled and waved as I rolled my suitcase out of the bar.

I boarded my flight, settled into my seat, and closed my eyes as I rested my head against the window. I was silently berating myself for not getting Tom's number. Even though I'm usually the first person to blow off a romantic connection, I felt like he was…*different* somehow. I drifted off to sleep thinking about his blue eyes and cute dimples.

MJ had a sign for me and was waiting at the gate when my plane landed. I ran to her, so excited when I saw the sign that I couldn't stop smiling. We hugged, and she grabbed my hand and pulled me towards the exit. "We have three days of fun ahead of us, girl. Ready, set, go!" We were like two schoolgirls having a play date for the first time.

"Okay, Daddy wants to take us to dinner tonight at the club. I told him I wasn't sure if we would commit and that I would have to talk to you first and see what you think?"

I had missed MJ's energy. "Seriously, he wants to buy us dinner, and you said you had to *think* about it? How about we go to dinner with your dad at the club, and then we go out afterwards?"

"Oh my goodness, he's going to be thrilled. He's been dying to meet you. A bunch of my family will be out there, too, because my cousin is coming home from Costa Rica today. He was doing missionary work out there for a year, but my mom says it was just an excuse for him to go surfing. He's a tool, but it would be good to see him. You sure you're okay with all of this?"

"I'm up for anything! I am just so glad to be here. I don't care what we do."

MJ's apartment was adorable. She lived in a nice retirement community and was the youngest person residing there by about fifty years. Her grandmother had passed away with six more years prepaid on her lease, so MJ's dad had just moved her things in before she came home from TWA. He hired a decorator to spruce up the place and bought her all new furniture. Everything looked as though it came right out of *Southern Living* magazine. MJ had wicker furniture on her porch with huge throw pillows and pretty flowers everywhere. The colors throughout the apartment were blue and yellow, and the atmosphere was cozy.

"Megan, do you want some iced tea? We can drink it out on the porch."

"That sounds great. I love this apartment, and you have it decorated so cute. I feel like Martha Stewart is going to walk out of the bathroom any minute. You look like you've got everything figured out."

MJ started laughing, "You're a nut job, but I love you to death. You know why you can't seem to "figure anything out"? One: You talk about it too much. And two: Stop complaining and do something about it. You over analyze everything, which goes hand-in-hand with number one. Just work on making yourself the best you can be and quit thinking about how miserable you are. You have so many talents, and people are automatically drawn to you. Think about precious Ted from TWA. Every girl had a crush on him, and he asked *you* out. He wanted to date *you*. He told me that he was in love with you. You have to learn to let people in your life like you have let me. You have serious trust issues that you *have* to get over, sweet child of mine."

"I know, I've got issues; we studied people like me in my psych classes." We both laughed. "Oh! I almost forgot to tell you! I met the cutest guy today at the airport in Charlotte during my layover. Talk about precious! I can still see his piercing blue eyes."

"Oooooh, what was his name?"

"Tom. I know his first name was Tom, but I can't remember his last name."

"Tom? Hmmmmm. Where was he going?"

"He said he was going home, but I didn't ask where home was. I don't have a clue where he's from or what his last name is. I probably met the man of my dreams today, and I won't ever see him again. I didn't even think to get a way to contact him. And you think I'm *smart*?"

"Actually, I think I called you a nut job." MJ's phone started ringing.

"Hello? Oh, hey, Daddy." She listened to her dad on the phone.

"Yes, Daddy, she's here. We are drinking iced tea on the porch." She paused. "Okay, we will see you in about an hour. I love you, too."

MJ hung up the phone and gave me the low down. "Okay, we have to leave here in about thirty minutes because Daddy wants us to stop by my cousin's welcome home party first. Then we're having dinner."

"What should I wear?" I asked as I got up from the porch and started to rummage through my suitcase.

"Come on, let's check out my closet and see what fits. You can pick out anything you want."

"I have died and gone to heaven."

"You're so easy to please," MJ replied as I followed her to her room.

When we pulled up to the country club, it was the epitome of old money, elegance, and Southern charm. I felt like I had just stepped into a scene from *Gone with the Wind*. The front porch was covered with huge ferns, rocking chairs, beautiful flowers, and enormous white columns. Black hurricane shutters stood out against the brick, accentuated by ornate lights. The country club was located right on the water with boats docked behind the exquisite plantation house. I thought I was dreaming as I took in the picturesque manicured lawns and the moss hanging from the trees. We walked into the main foyer, and two servers greeted us. They escorted us into the ballroom where the party was being held. Twenty people or so were scattered throughout the room that overlooked the Beaufort River. The view was breathtaking; however, it was another sight that made me stop abruptly. My eyes locked on a familiar face I had first seen earlier that day.

"Oh my gosh, MJ! That's the guy from the airport. Holy shit, I can't believe it."

"You see Tom?" She asked, grinning.

"No! It's the french fry guy. How do you know him? Tell me that isn't your cousin!"

"Richard? How do you know Richard? I thought you met a guy named Tom?"

"I did, I did. Before that, though, there was this annoying guy that was harassing me at the bar. He wanted me to eat one of his fries. It was very bizarre. I told him I was fasting for world hunger, so he would leave me alone. Is he your cousin that just came back from Costa Rica?"

"Yep, and nobody likes him. He probably hasn't been taking his meds, so he might be a little more off than usual. He's certifiable and has this weird obsession with skinny women. That's probably why he messed with you today. I knew we shouldn't have come. I think Daddy wanted us here because he was afraid no one else would show up. Let's find him and get the heck out of here."

"I'm going to the ladies room. I'll meet you in the hallway. I want to get out of here now before Richard sees me." I turned around briskly and made it to the ladies room in the clear. I knocked my wrist on my leg when I reached for the door handle and my bracelet fell off. *I really should get this clasp fixed*, I thought to myself as I bent over to pick it up. When I stood back up, I bumped into one of the waiters from the main dining room.

"Pardon me," he said, stopping for a moment. " Oh, you must be MJ's friend. Are you Megan?"

"Yeah, I am. How did you know that?" I asked, surprised.

"Beaufort is very small, and I'm a friend of hers. She's been talking about you ever since she came back from TWA. We're supposed to meet up with you guys at the Blind Tiger tonight. I'm Billy. It's nice to meet you. MJ didn't tell me how cute you are."

"Gosh, thanks." I grinned as I felt heat on my cheeks. "It was nice meeting you. I guess I'll see you later."

"Yeah, see you tonight." He turned around and headed towards the main dining room.

I walked into the bathroom and looked at myself in the mirror. I smiled at myself and turned my head from side to side. I wrinkled my nose, dissatisfied with my reflection. I pulled a tube of lipstick from my purse and applied it, thinking I could use a little color in my face. I stepped back from the mirror, only to find that the shade of lipstick MJ let me borrow is definitely *not* my color. *Too late now,* I thought as I walked out the door.

MJ was waiting for me in the lobby with her dad, and he was nothing like I thought he'd be. I pictured a tall, dark, and slender gentleman who resembled the Marlboro Man, but instead, he resembled Colonel Sanders without the mustache. He was wearing a light blue seersucker suit and greeted me with a warm bear hug. He thanked me for being such a good friend to his "little sugar plum." He gave MJ a couple of bills and told us to have a good time, and not to hesitate to call him if we needed a ride home. He even apologized for his obnoxious nephew.

We went to one of MJ's favorite restaurants. The food was delicious. I had never eaten shrimp and grits, and I literally licked my plate clean. I always knew MJ loved grits, but I had no idea how much I needed them in my life. For some reason, I had never understood the fascination, but I did after that meal. I had been in the South less than six hours, and I had already become a true Southerner (at least by my definition). MJ also introduced me to her favorite drink, a mint julep, and it became my new best friend. I felt like a true Southern woman drinking my mint julep and eating shrimp and grits. I could've sworn I was developing an accent.

When we finished dinner, we headed to the Blind Tiger. We had heard an awesome band was supposed to be playing. MJ knew everyone in town, and I felt like a celebrity when we walked into the bar. People made their way over to us and introduced themselves. Billy showed up, and I overheard him telling MJ that he could make my dreams come true. I decided it was time to find the bathroom at that point. Their conversation was about to get too deep for me.

When I walked out of the bathroom, there was a fight going on, and I stepped to the right to avoid the chaos. Billy came over with my drink and was talking his head off. I realized I'd had one too many mint juleps, and my eyes were starting to cross. I was pushed to the floor by a surge of people behind me. As I tried to gather my bearings, I felt a hand come down and lift me up. I wasn't sure who it was, but he knew my name.

"Thanks, I really appreciate the lift," I said and giggled at my new friend. But once I made eye contact, my mouth dropped open. I'd recognize those blue eyes anywhere. Tom.

"Hey, you. You look like you could use some help and maybe some coffee?" He grinned.

"What? I mean, how? I mean, what are you *doing* here?" I said in total disbelief.

"I live here. I wanted to tell you today, but you cut me off when you were heading to your flight. Well, our flight. I sat four rows behind you and saw you sleeping when I boarded the plane. I didn't want to wake you, and you were so happy when you saw MJ with the sign that I just figured I'd talk to you later. I'm not one of those people you were afraid you were going to run into today, am I? You know, one of those annoying people that you might continually see throughout the weekend?"

We both just smiled at each other and didn't say anything. I couldn't gather any words to form a sentence. I was speechless, just grinning from ear to ear.

"I did tell you that Beaufort was a small town, didn't I? And Billy isn't the right guy for you, if you ask me. I mean, you *are* asking me, right?"

"Yes," I tried to answer, but I was having trouble putting words together. I cleared my throat and said, "Yes, I'm asking."

"You know, you seem like you've have had a lot to drink. Since I'm a good Southern boy, I'm going to take you and MJ home right now.

"You know MJ?"

"Yep, we've been best friends since we were kids. Our moms were friends, so we grew up together. I went to the country club because MJ told me to meet y'all there, but I heard you had already left. I've been looking all over town for you two."

"Okay, Billy and all of these random people know who I am from MJ's stories. If you're her *best friend*, you had to have known she was the friend I was visiting. Why didn't you tell me you knew her when I talked to you at the airport?"

"Well, when I realized who you were, I was hoping I'd make an impression. Then I could run into you again and surprise you. Did it work?"

"I haven't been able to get you out of my head," I replied.

"Same for me. Come on, let's find MJ and get you guys out of here. You need to sleep this off."

"Well, you're a little forward, but I'm really okay with that," I laughed as he pulled me through the bar to find MJ.

"It's a good thing my momma raised me right because I could take advantage of this situation."

"You gotta love a momma's boy!"

"That's what my momma says." He smiled as he motioned to MJ to meet us outside.

The next morning, I woke up to MJ and Tom drinking coffee on her porch. My head ached, and I was so thirsty I couldn't even swallow. I walked to the kitchen, filled a huge glass with water, drank it, and filled it back up again. I tried to check out my reflection in the microwave door and realized there was no use. I walked out to the patio, and they started clapping their hands.

"Good morning, sunshine! How are you feeling?" MJ squealed at a decibel that was way too high for my liking.

"Not so good. What the heck is in those Mint Tulips or whatever it was that I was drinking? Maybe I wasn't meant to be a Southerner, after all." I covered my face with my hands, not wanting to make eye contact with Tom. I tried to fix my hair with my fingers.

They both laughed. MJ got up and said she was going to run to McDonald's to get breakfast for us. I definitely needed something greasy. She left me alone with Tom. All I could remember from the night before was that MJ and Tom were best friends.

I finally looked at Tom and said, "Hi."

He moved over next to me and said, "Hi."

"I'm so sorry for my behavior last night. You must think I'm the biggest loser in the entire world. So with that said, I'm going to take a shower. I'll see you later when I can hold my eyes open in the light."

"Okay, sounds good. MJ said that y'all are coming to my house for dinner tonight, so I'll see you around six-ish."

He leaned close and whispered in my ear, "I promise I won't have any mint *tulips*...just water if that makes you feel better. And for the record, you look more beautiful now than when I saw you at the airport." He kissed my forehead and walked out of the apartment.

I sat on the sofa thinking to myself, *what just happened?* When MJ came back with breakfast I sat her down and drilled her with questions about Tom. She told me that he was twenty-six years old, the town bachelor, extremely wealthy, and that every girl wanted to date him, but he wasn't interested in anyone. She told me that she had secretly been planning on fixing me up with him and thought that we would be perfect together. I guess she had told him, but neglected to tell me, about the potential fix up.

"You know how when someone fixes you up, you feel like a loser? I didn't want you to think that you couldn't find your own boyfriend. I just wanted to give you a little push in the right direction. Tom is a total catch, Megan. Do not let your stupid issues ruin this for you. As your friend, I'm telling you not to run away. Just give it a chance. I promise, you won't regret it."

"Okay, I hear what you're saying. I know I should trust you, but how can I do that when you had me drinking those God forsaken mint tulips?" I started to laugh but had to stop because it hurt my head. "For real, what the hell is in those drinks?"

"Bourbon, and it kicks your butt, doesn't it? Eat your egg McMuffin and drink your coke. You've got to sleep it off. Tonight's going to be a big night for you."

Dinner was great. Tom entertained us while he cooked. We talked about his cotton business, the family farm, his parents, and his love for the ocean. After dinner, MJ went home, and Tom and I strolled down to the Southern Sweets Ice Cream Parlor and ate the best vanilla ice cream I had ever had. We sat on the bench swings at the Waterfront Park and looked out over the water. The night was clear and a light breeze kept us cool as we got to know each other.

The next two days were like a dream. I loved being in a small town where people passed by on their boats and waved to their neighbors. I felt more at home than I had anywhere else in a very long time.

Tom came over to say good-bye the night before I left. He sat with MJ and me on her porch and listened to our stories about Allison from TWA. He kept asking how he could get in touch with her.

"Get in line," I said. "There were guys who heard about Allison and asked me out just to go back to my room.

"Hey, did you tell Megan your news?" Tom asked MJ.

"No, I didn't," she replied. I could see how uncomfortable she felt.

"What's the news, MJ?"

"I have an interview with Delta Airlines in Atlanta next week. I applied about six months ago, and I've had two interviews so far. One was a phone interview, and the other was here in town about three weeks ago. I didn't say anything because I wasn't sure how you'd feel about the whole thing."

"Wow, that's awesome! I'm so happy for you. You know, this is so much better for you than that mortician job."

Tom and MJ laughed. MJ's phone rang, so she went inside to answer it.

Tom put his arm around my shoulder and said, "I've gotta go, Megan. Why don't you walk me out to my truck?"

"How could I refuse those dimples? Lead the way."

We walked out through MJ's front door. Tom was talking, but I was deep in thought. I realized that I liked how I felt about myself when I was with him. I felt like he could see right through me. The thing that always scared me about dating was that I was afraid of being discarded, of being left alone. I didn't want the uncertainty of investing in someone and then have him leave. Ever since my mother died, I had ruined every relationship because I wanted to control it. But I realized that wasn't getting me any farther along in life. I had been alone for six years, and I wasn't any better. I wasn't happy, and I wasn't making sound life decisions. I decided I wanted to lead with my heart this time. I finally felt ready to open up to someone. But then I realized we were already at Tom's truck, and I hadn't heard a word he had said.

"So what do you think?" Tom smiled at me and flashed his dimples.

I didn't have a clue what he was saying. "What do *you* think?" I asked, thinking I'd get some sort of hint.

"I don't think you were listening to me, so I'm going to decide for you. Sound good?"

I couldn't help but laugh. He had my ticket. "I'm not sure that's a good idea. I mean, I might need some more information before I can trust you!"

"Nope, it's settled. You have one year. I'll call you tomorrow night to make sure you got home okay. I've got paper in my truck, so you can write your number down for me." He pulled a pen out of his glove compartment and handed me a piece of paper. I still had no idea what kind of agreement we had made, and he was obviously enjoying my ignorance. We said our good-byes, and he told me that he'd see me in two weeks. *Two weeks?* I thought. *What?*

He advised me to study hard in school and to stay away from mint tulips. I couldn't help but laugh as he drove away because he officially had my heart. I saw it in the back seat of the truck waving at me, happy it had a new home. Life was good.

MJ was hired at Delta Airlines and was traveling the world like we had planned to do. I, on the other hand, was pursuing an elementary education degree back in Dayton. Although I had changed my major about a thousand times, I finally had a goal and worked harder than I ever had in my life. I was averaging twenty-three hours each quarter at school and working three part-time jobs. I had special permission from the Dean of the college every quarter to take so many hours. Tom came to visit every two weeks, and he flew me down to see him when he couldn't get away. He became the best friend I needed, a coach that inspired me to be better, and the love of my life. MJ was right. He was the best thing that had ever happened to me.

A year had passed since we met. From the beginning, neither of us had dated anyone else, and he was in town for my graduation. We were eating dinner with Dad and Fiona, celebrating my graduation and the fact that I had made the Dean's list. After dinner, Tom told Dad about a promise he made to me in the parking lot of MJ's apartment on the first weekend I had met him. Fiona was talking about her internship in DC, and I immediately stopped her because I still didn't have a clue what he had said that night. Several times over the year, the conversation came up, but he would never tell me. I turned to him as he pulled out a ring box and put it on the table. My mouth dropped. I took a gulp of my wine and elbowed Fiona to make sure what I was seeing was really happening. She did a double take and reached for her glass, as well.

"Mr. O'Malley, I told Megan that she was the girl I was going to marry a year ago in that parking lot, but I told her she had to finish school before we'd get engaged. She did, and I am so proud of her." He put two fingers on the box and slid it over to me on the table. He smiled at me, lifted his fingers off the box, and motioned for me to look inside. My heart skipped a beat and then started hammering so hard, I thought it was going to pop out of my chest. Was this really happening? Fiona pinched my arm just so I knew I wasn't dreaming. My hand was shaking as I opened the box. Tom got down on one knee, "I promise to love, adore, and take care of you for the rest of my life. Will you marry me, Megan O'Malley?"

Of course my first reaction was to cry. Big surprise. I was thrilled that Tom chose to share this moment with my father and my sister. I had no doubt that he was the man for me. I knew I was lucky to have found him, but I also couldn't help but think of all the things that wouldn't be the same without my mom.

❖❖❖❖❖❖❖❖❖❖❖❖❖❖

I must have waited about thirty minutes when I finally saw a familiar woman walking towards me with my red purse. She smiled and asked if I went to Stella Maris Catholic Church on Sullivan's Island. We talked for a couple of minutes about church, and I thanked her. "See you at nine-thirty mass on Sunday," I said.

I walked out the front door of the airport, turned to my left, and saw Tom's blue Ford Flex near the baggage claim. He saw me and pulled up beside me, then jumped out to greet me with a huge bear hug. I didn't want to let go because I had been through so much since I had seen him four nights ago in our bedroom.

"Are you healed?" He joked as he put the car in drive.

"Yes and no...but definitely more yes than no," I told him.

He smiled, "Well that explains the puffy eyes."

"Tom, they look so much better. Trust me."

Chapter Twenty-Four
Flowers

Two weeks had passed since the trip, and I was in a good place. I hadn't shed any tears. That was a huge deal, if you ask me. I started my summer job as a receptionist at the hair salon; the kids were enjoying their summer vacation; and Tom and I were making time for one another. He was teaching me to stand up paddleboard, and we were having fun. After our lessons on Sullivan's Island, we would head to Poe's and have a couple of beers to celebrate my success. I had gained more insight into my life and the journey I was on. I forgave myself for being an insensitive teenager when Mom was sick; I forgave myself for not being a better sister to Fiona; and I realized that my mom had loved me despite my faults and ignorance of her needs. I saw more than ever how important it was to be a great mom to my own children and a better wife to Tom. I'm not so sure why it took so long for me to accept it, but I guess I needed to face my past in order to understand it. Going through my childhood home, spending time with Uncle John, and visiting my mother's grave made me realize things I hadn't known before the trip. I hadn't known that Mom and Uncle John had a special relationship, like Helen's and Fiona's. They share a beautiful and nurturing love for each other that only exists when a sibling steps in to serve in the absence of a mother. I realized that the love of family is a blessing. I learned to treasure it and cherish it because everyone isn't so lucky to have it.

On Sunday morning about seven-thirty, my phone beeps. It's a text from Fiona telling me to check my e-mail. I pour myself another cup of coffee and turn on my laptop. The house is quiet, and no one else is awake. I love mornings like this when I can slowly wake up and gather my thoughts.

I walk out on the back porch with my computer, so I can enjoy being outside before the temperature skyrockets. I click on my e-mail icon and see a message from Uncle John.

Hello Girls,

Hope everybody is doing fine. I met with Murphy and your dad this week. We had a great time, but my golf game sucked. It was really bad. Fiona would have buried me, but my excuse is that I had the flu and hadn't eaten in four days. So after four holes, my energy level was low. (Maybe.)

As promised I went to the cemetery to check on the rocks and here is my report.

A little purple flower is now growing beside the three rocks you placed by your mother's gravestone. It is delicate and beautiful. I didn't look for your note, Megan, because I didn't want to be tempted to read it. I know it was meant for your mother. It must still be there because the ground doesn't look like it has been disturbed. The six rocks we placed around the tree are still there, as well. I'm sure your mother loves it.

Good job, girls. It's a great tribute to Ginny.

Have a great rest of the summer.

Uncle J

I read the e-mail five times. Tears came like a fountain. I knew what the flower meant. I thought of my mother praying the novena and then crying over roses she received when her chemo wasn't working. Twenty-five years later, we had prayed the novena at her grave and now a flower was growing just where we had stood.

Maybe I am more like Mom than I thought, I think to myself. I had been so good about not crying, but I had prayed for this sign. I believed this was a sign from Mom to tell me that she loved me and that she was proud of me. I read the e-mail again and tried to picture what the flower looked like, but it didn't matter. The flower was a miracle in my mind.

I immediately called Helen, but she didn't answer. I looked at my watch and realized she probably wasn't even awake yet. I called Fiona, and she didn't answer her phone either. I decided to get ready for mass and try again later. The kids and I headed to church, and I couldn't stop thinking about the flower. They were talking in the car and asking me questions, but it all jumbled together. I was thinking of my mom. *She loves me, and she's proud of me.* I looked at myself in the rear view mirror and smiled.

The kids and I entered Stella Maris Church on Sullivan's Island, and I had goose bumps on my arms. Entering the church always gives me an overwhelming feeling of peace, but this morning, I felt happy. During the entrance hymn, I tried to sing along, but I kept thinking of the flower and had to fight back happy tears. All through mass, I thought about my prayer. I got my sign. I actually felt like she was talking to me.

When we visited, there was nothing but dirt and grass all around Mom's grave. The only flowers that were around were the ones that the landscapers had planted or decorative plants loved ones had put on other graves. I kept thinking about how dry the dirt was that day and that Uncle John had mentioned it hadn't rained in a while. It truly was a miracle that such a beautiful flower was growing right from the rocks. I felt like it was my mom's way of wrapping her arms around us and giving us a huge hug.

Four days later, my sister-in-law sent me a picture. She and my brother Murphy were in Dubuque for a reunion, and they had gone to visit my mother's grave to see the rocks. In the picture, a lavender wildflower was growing from the rocks we had placed, just like Uncle John said it was. But three blooms were also sprouting. Seeing the picture, I knew the three blooms represented Helen, Fiona, and me. This was Mom's way of saying she was with us. *Typical of Mom to always have the last word. That's just part of the role of a mother,* I think. *Once a mom, always a mom. No matter where you go.*

I immediately initiated a three-way conference call with Helen and Fiona. Fiona was moved, like I was, but Helen was more of a doubting Thomas. She felt it had value, but didn't feel the connection that Fiona and I did. We didn't press it and talked about a couple of other things before we ended the phone call. After talking to the girls, my excitement didn't dwindle. I knew that flower was for us, and nothing anyone could say, even doubting Thomas, was going to make me think differently.

Two weeks later, Helen called me somewhat excited, almost out of breath.

"Megan, I was backing out of the driveway on my way to mass with the kids this morning, and I noticed something lavender growing on the hedge along the back of the our yard. You know the one that everyone has? The subdivision is in charge of the maintenance. It's supposed to be like a fence since we back up to the main road. Anyway, it caught my eye because the hedge is green and the bloom was purple. So, when I got back from mass, I was drinking my coffee on the back porch and noticed the flower again. I walked over to look at it closer. Megan, we have lived in this house for thirteen years, and I have never seen a flower on the hedge like I saw today. It had three blooms. *Three blooms.* So, I decided to get my roller blades on and check out the entire neighborhood for a blooming flower in the hedge. Guess what. There wasn't another flower like this in the entire neighborhood! I probably spent two hours on my skates hoping to find another flower like the one in my yard growing from the hedge, but I didn't see one *anywhere*. I think this flower was for me, and I think it's a sign from Mom."

We talked for an hour. She sent me a picture of the flower via text, and it was beautiful. The hedge was green and thriving, and then this beautiful flower with three blooms stands out like a diamond in the rough. I agree with her that it's another sign from Mom. "She knew she had to put it in your yard to make you notice because you've always been stubborn and tenacious. Since you weren't that impressed with the flowers at her grave, she brought the flower to you," I told her.

About a week later, Fiona called with a flower spotting in her yard. She and her husband plant red geraniums around the front of their house every year because the house is white, and they want some contrasting color. Her husband Sterling was a landscaper years ago and has always done a great job with their yard. The grass is kept, the flowerbeds are well maintained, and you can tell they take pride in their yard. The backyard is probably my favorite part because it's perfect for football games and parties. I love the Irish wall they built in the very back of the yard. Anyway, a three-foot cement wall supports the driveway of the neighbor's house next door. It starts at the foot of the neighbor's driveway and goes straight down Fiona's yard. I think for a while it was a bit of an eyesore, but Sterling planted some wildflowers and the beautiful, vibrant colors practically hide it. Every morning, weather permitting, Fiona and Sterling drink their coffee outside on the patio. Sterling usually finishes first and walks around the yard feeding wild rabbits, putting out nuts for the squirrels, and checking on his plants. Fiona makes fun of him and calls him the "Bird Whisperer" since he is so in tune with the wildlife in their backyard.

While he was making his daily rounds that morning, he noticed a lavender flower with three blooms that he had never seen before. He knew he hadn't planted them and called Fiona over to ask if she knew anything about them. She shook her head in disbelief. She had noticed them the same time Sterling did and was completely taken back. She felt that it was a sign of her own. Three separate blooms of the same flower? The flowers at the grave, the flowers at Helen's, and now flowers in her yard couldn't be a coincidence. After the flowers bloomed for a couple of days, neither Helen nor Fiona saw the flowers in their yards again.

Chapter Twenty-Five
I'm Going to Need Time

The following Saturday, Tom and I had just finished another paddleboard lesson at 30th Avenue on Sullivan's Island, and he twisted my arm to grab a beer at Poe's. We loaded the paddleboards, wiped the sand off our feet, and headed that way. We walked through the picket fence and picked out a table with an umbrella to give us a little shade. As soon as we sat down, the waitress got our drink orders and dropped off menus. I put both elbows on the table and flashed my best smile at Tom. He looked at me and said, "I'm not sure who you are, but I think you're still in shock from that shark!"

I put my hands over my face, my elbows resting on the table, like I was trying to hide from the memory of what I saw in the water. "You might have set me back a couple of years in therapy after seeing that shark today. Had I seen it when I was on the paddleboard, I seriously would have had a heart attack. I'm already afraid of the water. I didn't need that shark to add to it."

"Megan, come on. It was a baby shark, and it was *dead*."

"But it was alive when you first saw it swimming by me, right? And you were a little nervous because you were walking up and down the beach, watching the shark as it was watching me."

"Megan, he wasn't *watching* you. I knew something was wrong with the little guy because he was swimming funny. He wasn't going to hurt you," Tom said as he smiled at the waitress who had returned with our beers.

"Right…right…right…." I said sarcastically. "That fin is going to haunt me."

"Y'all ready to order, or do you need a couple of minutes?"

173

"I'm going to have the Gold Bug burger with cheddar cheese, lettuce, tomato, mayo on the side, and fries. Can you cook that medium-well for me?"

The waitress nodded her head as she was writing my order. She turned to Tom and asked, "And for you?"

"I'll have the mahi mahi tacos."

"Okay, I'll get that in right away."

"Oh, can I get a glass of water when you get a chance?" I asked.

"No problem."

"Thanks."

The waitress took the menus and went to place the order. We sat there quietly for a couple of minutes watching the palm trees sway in the wind and sipping on our beers. When you've been married for seventeen years, sometimes quiet is a good thing. You aren't complaining or nagging your spouse—just enjoying the silence. (Not that I *ever* nag or complain.)

There always seems to be so much noise at our house. Music blaring at high volumes; Ginny listens to country, and Liam likes rock. The television is loud because no one can hear it over the music that's playing upstairs, and Seth is always yelling for something he either needs or can't find in the house. He always forgets to get a towel when he takes a shower, or he doesn't have any toilet paper in the bathroom. So, needless to say, the silence was a good thing. It was such a beautiful afternoon, and we were soaking in the good vibrations all around us. Tourists were walking by, people were going to and from the beach, and vacationers were having some harmless fun at Dunlevy's Bar across the street. Poe's has always been one of our favorite places because we love the food and the location. We usually sit outside. The locals and tourists wear a uniform of swimsuits, board shorts, flips flops, and sunglasses. You can always smell suntan lotion in the air, and when the wind blows just the right way, you can smell the marsh from the inter-coastal waters about three blocks behind the restaurant. Not to mention the sounds of seagulls flying overhead. I love where we live. I think to myself that I should convince Helen and Fiona to do a sisters' trip here.

"You look good, Megan. I mean you look happy. It's like something is different about you, and I can't figure it out," Tom said.

I pulled the empty chair next to me out, so I could put my feet up to get more comfortable. I grabbed my beer off the table and said, "You know, I *feel* happy for the first time in a really long time." I took a sip of my beer and watched a woman who was pushing a stroller down the street. Then I leaned forward and put my beer back on the table. "Wait, let me rephrase that," I corrected myself as I took my sunglasses off and placed them on the table. "I'm happy because I don't feel guilty anymore about the way I treated my mother." I tucked my hair behind my ears and thought about what I wanted to say. "That trip was healing in so many ways. I don't think I'll ever be able to process it completely, but it changed my life."

"I can really see it. I just wish you and your sisters did this years ago. Why is it that no one listens to me?"

"Because you're wrong ninety-five percent of the time, and I say that with the utmost respect, honey. I mean who would have thought you'd be right about this one? Seriously, Tom, I'm completely aware of your limitations."

We both laughed because he knew I was kidding. Or was I? I'll never tell.

My phone rang, and I moved my feet off the chair to grab my purse. I looked at the caller ID and saw that it was Fiona. "Hey, Fiona, what's up?"

"Tell Fiona I said 'hi,'" Tom said. "I'm going to the bathroom. How about ask the waitress to get another beer for me."

I nod, "Okay. Fiona, Tom says 'hi.'"

"Hey, I just got off the phone with Helen, and we were thinking about our trip for next year. We thought that maybe we should come to Charleston, and Tom could take the kids somewhere for a couple days so we could stay at your house? What do you think? Helen could drive from Florida, and I could get a cheap flight, and Suson could drive too. You have the beaches, cool restaurants downtown, and that fun golf cart that we can drive to bars in your neighborhood. What do you think?"

"Fiona, it's perfect! Tom and I are here at Poe's having a late lunch, and I was thinking the same thing. Definitely, let's plan on it."

"Okay, it's settled. I have to run because Sterling and I are meeting Dad at the country club for golf today. The Bird Whisperer got a little carried away this morning with feeding all the wild animals in the yard, and now we're running late."

"Okay, can you Skype tonight? I'll call Helen, and we can all have a glass of wine together around seven-thirty. How does that sound?" I asked.

"Sounds good. Talk to you tonight."

"Bye."

Tom came back to the table, "Did you order me another beer?"

"No, the waitress never came back. Wait, here she comes with our food."

"Okay, the Gold Bug burger for you, and the mahi mahi tacos for you. Can I get you two another beer?" She asked as she placed our food in front of us.

"I've got everything I need." I smiled as I thought about what I had said. "But he would like one please?"

"Okay, enjoy your meal," the waitress said as she walked to another table.

"So what did Fiona want?" Tom asked, trying to figure out how to pick up his taco without losing everything in it.

"She thought we should do our sisters' trip here next summer, and I thought that was a great idea. I love the fact that I wouldn't have to travel, and the best part is that I would get to be a tourist in my own town. You know, do things I never get to do."

"I'm assuming that I'm going to have to take the kids somewhere for a couple of days while they're here?"

"Unless you want to spend three full days with my sisters...?"

"Yeah, I think we can go to my brother's and go out on the boat."

"Keith would love that, don't you think?" I asked.

"Yeah, and the kids will have a ball," Tom declared.

"Perfect, it's a plan," I said as I raised my beer. "Cheers."

"I hope you're that happy when I tell you that I don't have my wallet," Tom laughed.

"You're lucky that shark didn't get me, you know that?"

"If that shark got you, Megan, I'd be at the Jammer at the bikini contest."

"You really know how to hide your emotions, Tom. I know you're still in shock from the shark."

"Right, right, right. Do you have enough money for me to get another beer?"

"I think I need another one now. Order me one, too," I said.

Tom laughed. He got up from his chair, leaned over, and kissed me on my cheek. "I love you, Bo Bo. I wouldn't know what to do without you."

I smiled at him and told him he was an idiot. He responded, "Babe, that's why you love me."

I picked up my beer, took another sip, and thought, *he's right, that is why I married him. He always makes me laugh. I really hate it when he's right.*

When we got home and walked into the house, Seth was yelling from the downstairs bathroom that he didn't have any toilet paper, Ginny was in the shower singing at the top of her lungs, and Liam was jamming out to the Red Hot Chili Peppers in his bedroom upstairs. I took the stack of mail on the counter out to the porch. Tom went to get toilet paper for Seth from our bathroom, and told Liam to turn down the music. He also banged on the bathroom door to tell Ginny to hurry up and quit wasting water, knowing she takes thirty-minute showers.

"I went to the beach with Isabelle, and I can't get the sunscreen out of my hair," she yelled.

Tom came back downstairs and met me on the porch with the toilet paper in hand. We heard the cry of a desperate little boy in the background, "I can't feel my legs anymore! Can somebody *please* bring me toilet paper?!"

"I'll be right back," he said. I continued looking through the mail. I heard Tom walk through the kitchen and knock on the bathroom door. He told Seth, "Son, check the toilet paper before you sit on the commode."

I laughed to myself and put the bills in one pile and the junk mail in another. Tom came back to the porch, sat down next to me, and asked if there was anything good in the mail.

"Yes, if you like bills and junk mail, you're in luck."

"Not so much. Did I see my surfing magazine?"

"Yep, I put it in the junk mail pile." I waited for his reaction.

"*What?*" He panicked, frantically searching through the pile. "That's sacrilegious! Don't ever do that to my surfing magazine. There's no respect," he muttered.

"Hey, I have to talk to you about something, and I need your full attention, okay?"

"Uh oh. What did I do?" He put his head down as if he was ready for his punishment.

I laughed. "You didn't do anything. I want to do something, but I'm going to need your help. Well, maybe not your help, but definitely your support."

"You can go to Belk, just put it on the thirty-sixty-ninety, so we don't pay any interest," he said as he got up and turned to walk back into the house.

"That's not it. But wait? You don't care if I go to Belk?" I think about that for a minute before I tell him what I really want. *He never gives me a hall pass to go to Belk,* I think to myself. *Maybe I should just take the card and forget about my idea? No, I don't think I can let this go.*

I'm losing my focus, so I just come out and say it.

"I want to write a book about my mom." I pause for a moment and let him comprehend what I'm saying. He came back out and sat down across from me.

"I think that's a great idea. What do you need from me?"

I smiled and said, "Time. I'm going to need time to write it, and I'm going to need help with the kids and the house."

"I'll help, but you can't get upset when it isn't done *exactly* the way you want it done. Fair?" He was giving me a somewhat patronizing look, but I didn't care. I just wanted him to say he would support me.

I nodded my head and smiled at him.

"Now, I want to know why you feel the need to write about your mom?"

"I've been thinking about it a lot, especially since I got back from Iowa. I started thinking about how Helen, Fiona, Uncle John, and that trip pulled me to a new level of understanding and how I have been grieving for so long. I have been to both sides, Tom. Do you know what I mean by that?"

He gave me a confused look, "No, I don't have a clue what that means."

"It means that my whole life, I have felt cheated. Cheated about my mom dying; cheated about the time I didn't get to spend with her; cheated about the times I needed a mother, and she wasn't there. But after being at her grave and standing there as a mother myself, close to the age that she was when she died, I contemplated everything differently than I had before. For example, first and foremost, I realized that *Mom* was the one who was cheated. She didn't have any memories of her mother because she was two years old when her mom died. I *have* memories. Beautiful memories of her with my dad, of our family, and of talks that she and I had together. Tom, I had birthdays where she made me a special dinner. I have the memory of her Christmas cookies that we all fought over every Christmas Eve. Every Easter, she made me a new dress, and she let me pick out the pattern and fabric. I have wonderful memories of family vacations when we went to the beach. She didn't have *any* of that. The part that haunts me is that she knew what it was like to grow up without a mother, and she *knew* that her own children would have to suffer through the same thing. She knew when she looked at Fiona and me that she would never see us graduate from high school or college. She would never see us get married. She would never know any of her grandchildren. I may not have realized she was dying, and maybe that was my fault; maybe it wasn't. That part doesn't matter now. But she did. She *knew*. She died knowing it. I can't even imagine what that was like. Standing at her grave, I thought about what it would be like to know I was dying and leaving you and the kids behind, and it broke my heart. So, do you understand now what I mean when I say I've been to both sides?"

"Wow, you have really thought about this, haven't you?"

"And I want to write about how the rocks, paper, and flowers helped me through the process. Fiona was right about the rocks. They helped with the physical part of my healing. I took my pain and guilt with that rock, and I left it at the grave. Then I started thinking about all the rocks that I have in my life. People who care about me, the ones I know I can count on when life doesn't go as planned: like you, my sisters, my friends, and my other family. The letter I got from Amy that I buried was emotionally healing for me. I was so surprised. I didn't expect it, but it really helped me. Everything she wrote in that letter was what I wanted my mom to say to me. It's tattooed in my mind. I found my new perspective when I was standing at Mom's grave, as a mother myself, just a couple years shy of how old she was when she died. And the picture of the flowers that were growing right by the rocks we left at Mom's grave really sealed everything for me. I'm convinced that was Mom's way of saying everything is going to be okay. What do you think?"

Tom paused, then opened his mouth to reply. "Wait!" I yelled. "Before you say anything, I want to call it *Both Sides*. Okay, now what do you think?"

He looked at me with a half grin and said, "Go for it!"

Chapter Twenty-Six
Smile Like the Sun

One year later...

I walked inside the front door, sifting through the mail, and I heard, "Mom, Aunt Helen is on the phone for you!"

I stepped over to the kitchen counter and picked up the phone that Seth had answered for me. "Hey, Helen. Are you packed?"

"Of course not. I'm coming to The Collection in your closet. I'm not even sure I'm bringing my backpack," she laughed.

"Perfect, just bring a swimsuit and underwear. I've got everything else covered. What time are you leaving in the morning? Do you have to go into school?"

"Yeah, I have to stop by, but I should be on the road by eight-thirty. I plan on seeing you around three, just in time for happy hour."

"Sounds good. Fiona should get here around four-thirty, and Suson should be here around seven. I figured we could take the golf cart to High Thyme for dinner tomorrow night. There is something to be said about driving to dinner in a golf cart. You know, you really feel like you're on vacation. Call me during the drive and let me know how you're making it, okay?"

"I will, just have The Collection ready with a big glass of cabernet."

"Okay, see you tomorrow."

"Check ya later."

I hung up the phone and put the mail on the counter. I think to myself, *twenty-four hours and we all will be together again. I can't wait to be with my sisters. I can't wait to be in their company and talk about nothing of importance. I can't wait to wake up in the morning and drink coffee without any interruptions. I can't wait to have a Happy Hour with them that actually lasts for hours, and we laugh until we can't breathe. I can't wait to be with my sisters!* The sound of my husband's voice asking about dinner immediately pulls me from my daydream.

"I'm thinking breakfast food since I forgot to take meat out of the freezer?" I say as I'm still staring at the mail.

"Sounds good to me. Hey, did you check get mail?"

"It's right there on the counter, but I haven't really gone through it yet."

Tom walks over to the counter and sifts through it, "Junk mail, junk mail, bill, bill, bill, and you got a letter from your Uncle John."

"I did? Let me see it." I eagerly walk over to the counter and reach for the letter.

Tom handed it to me, and I ripped it open like it was a birthday present. I pulled out a chair from the kitchen table, sat down, and looked at the letter from my favorite cowboy. I was excited and a little nervous to read it because I had sent him a copy of my manuscript. I had sent nine months of my hard work to Uncle John, and he had promised to give me his opinion. I knew if he didn't like it, it would be a serious blow, and I wasn't sure I was ready for that kind of hit. Sadly enough, several publishing companies had rejected me already; nonetheless, it was important to me that he gave me his approval. I unfolded the letter.

Megan,

You're an amazing lady. I finished your story last evening before I had to leave to referee. You nailed the parts of the story in which I was involved. It was great to relive that wonderful weekend. It's one of the highlights of my life. And now it will be with me as long as I live. The story was great, but I want to answer a question you presented several times throughout it.

"What trait did I get from my mom?"

What trait did you get from your mom?

You gotta be kidding. I'll tell you.

For what at times were (or at least seemed like) good reasons, my family couldn't make it to Dubuque for family gatherings. Not actually good reasons, I guess. However, on the occasions that I did connect with Ginny after we had all moved away, our eyes would meet, and she would light up like the sun with a smile. We would then hug, and she would squeeze the wind from my lungs. We would give each other a kiss and then hug a little longer. She left no doubt in my mind I was very special and loved very much. It was a wonderful feeling. In my life, I have met many people. As a general rule, people like me, people respect me, people befriend me, but Ginny truly loved me. It was different, and it was good.

I remember meeting a darling little girl for the first time at my dad's home. At the time, she was Ginny's youngest daughter, and I fell in love with her. She's all grown up now, married and has a family, and is a talented and hard-working lady. I don't get to see her very often, but when I do, our eyes meet, she smiles like the sun, we hug, and she squeezes the air out of my lungs. We kiss and hug for a while longer. I truly feel loved by this woman, just as I did by my sister. If you haven't figured it out by now, this woman's name is Megan.

Megan, I wouldn't trade my relationship with you for all the gold in the world. This is the trait you received from your mother, and it is a very special gift. Helen and Murphy may have her courage and discipline. Jack may have her confidence and intelligence. Fiona and Shamus may have her sense of humor. But what you have, the ability to make someone feel loved, is very special. I'm sure your husband and children know this and love you very much. For the kids, it's a very tough time and decisions you make aren't always what they want to hear from you. But one day, they will be married with children, making decisions like you have to make today, and they will come and visit you. Your eyes will meet; they will smile like the sun; you will embrace in hugs; they will squeeze the air from your lungs; you will kiss and hug for a while longer. You will feel like the most loved person in the world because I know that's how you make them feel. And I know you have passed that trait on to them, and they will carry it with them always. Your mother was very special but not more special than you.

Well, I said what I wanted to say. Thank you for your kind words. One of these days, I will have to show you who I really am.

Your mother would be very proud but embarrassed with your wonderful tribute. It was very special for me to read. I loved it.

Great job!

Love you,

Uncle John

I read the letter over and over. It was the most beautiful thing I had ever read, and I couldn't believe it was about me. It was about *me*. Tears filled my eyes, and the lump in my throat was so big that it hurt. But I wasn't crying tears of sadness. I was crying tears of joy and relief, and tears of liberation. I always wanted to be told I was like my mother; I wanted some connection to her. Something…anything. But no one ever said I was like her. Maybe it was because I hadn't grown into the person I was meant to be yet. Regardless, for my whole life, I have tried to be the person she would want me to be, the type of person she would be proud to call her daughter. Then today, on just a typical, ordinary day, when I least expected it, I got a letter from one of the most treasured people in my mom's life. I finally had the answer to the question I had pondered for so long: the capacity to love and make others *feel* loved. That's what I share with my mother. I think to myself that I have the best trait of all. I have a special gift that's very powerful, especially for a mother. It's a gift that allows me to sift through the moodiness of a teenage daughter and know she doesn't mean it or cheer on a son at a baseball game and be the loudest fan in the crowd even when the going gets tough. This gift allows me to make three lunches in less than five minutes on a busy weekday morning, bake homemade cinnamon rolls on Saturday, and cry at every chorus performance because I'm overcome with the talent that happens to be my son and daughter. I have always been one to joke that it is better to receive than to give…but in this case, the more I give, the more I get back. I love, am loved, and I'm extremely lucky.

The next morning, Tom had the car packed for the trip to Uncle Keith's, and we all said our good-byes. The kids kissed my cheek and hugged my neck before they got in the car. "Have fun and please be careful. Don't forget to put on sunscreen, okay?" Everyone settled in, and Tom started the engine to get the air going full blast.

"We will!" Ginny yelled from the back seat. I glanced at Seth in the third seat. He had his headphones on and was listening to his iPod, ready to go. Liam was the co-pilot, trying to decide on a CD for the ride, and Ginny was reading her book. I leaned into the car and kissed Tom, "Call me when you get to Keith's, okay?"

"I will. Have fun with the sisters. Be sure to tell Fiona to wear flip flops in the shower." He laughed and pulled out of the driveway. I watched the car drive down the street until it was out of sight. *Safe travels,* I thought.

I walked back inside the house, and the phone was ringing. I looked at the caller ID. It was my friend Amy. "Hey, Amy. What's up? Are you in Atlanta, yet?"

"Hey, Megan…no I have a couple more hours to go, but I just wanted to tell you to have a great time with your sisters. I hate I can't meet up with you guys."

"I hate it, too, but you and your sister are going to have a ball! Enjoy yourself and do some shopping for me."

"Will do. Have you heard anything from the publishing company yet?"

"No, not yet, but that's okay. It's all about the journey, right? I've been consumed with the book for so long, and at this moment, until I hear something, I'm going to just focus on my sisters and goof off."

"Sounds good to me. Hey, my sister is on the other line. I should probably take this. I'll call you later. Have a great weekend."

"You, too! Check out the sale rack at Anthropologie for me!"

"Consider it done," she said as she laughed. "See you later."

"Bye, Amy."

I hung up the phone and bustled around the house making sure everything was ready for my guests. I went over my checklist: clean linens on the beds, fresh towels in the bathroom, coffee beans for the morning, and a couple of bottles of wine in the kitchen. *I have everything but snacks for Happy Hour and maybe I should get more wine? I probably should hop on the golf cart and head to the Piggly Wiggly for the snacks...maybe peanuts. Better yet, I should buy the girls some chocolate covered pecans from the Charleston Nut Company. The ferns are watered on the front porch; I've got beach chairs for the beach and lots of magazines that Helen will love.*

I decided to head to the store, so I hopped in the golf cart and drove to Piggly Wiggly. On my way back to the house, Helen called on my cell phone.

"Hi, Helen. Where are you?"

"Hey, Megan. I'm just outside of Jacksonville, Florida," she said kind of slowly. "Yep, I'm exactly twenty-three miles outside of Jacksonville, according to this sign."

"So you're about four hours away. I thought you would have been farther along than that?" I said as I tried to turn the golf cart into the driveway with one hand while I held the phone with the other.

"Well, I had a little delay because the front tire on my car keeps going flat. I called AAA, and they met me on the roadside and filled the tire with air. So, if I don't have any more problems, I should be there around four-thirty."

"Helen, has it happened more than once?" I asked, concerned.

"Well, first I found out the membership expired, so I had to renew my membership over the phone, then I waited like five minutes, called back, and I have used them twice since then."

I started laughing and said, "There has *got* to be a red flag next to your name at the AAA department."

"Let's hope not, since apparently I still have like four hours of driving before I get to your house. Oh, I don't have my phone charger because Colleen lost it, and I have to turn the phone off to save my battery. I will call you when I need you, okay?"

"Okay, be careful, Helen. I will have a huge glass of wine waiting for you when you get here."

"Okay, check ya later."

Apparently, she has everything under control, I thought to myself as I walked into the house with the groceries and gag gifts I had just purchased for the girls. I put the wine in the wine rack and wrapped the silly gifts. Helen had told me that lice and pinworms were running rampant in her classroom, and we laughed when I joked that I thought athlete's foot was the worst thing we could catch from our sister trips. I had purchased sweetgrass baskets for the girls and filled each of them with duct tape for pinworms, a bright flashlight to check for lice, chocolates because chocolate makes everything better, suntan lotion so we wouldn't burn, two magazines for the beach, and a tube of Preparation H. I read that it does wonders for puffy eyes, and Lord knows that after two days of no sleep, we will all need a little help. Oh, and a spray bottle of Tough Actin' Tinactin for Fiona and Suson. I knew they would get a kick out of them. Most hostesses give gifts of beauty or functional items, but in our family, we give humor. It's probably not the kind of humor that most people would understand, but it has been my saving grace throughout my whole life. It was the reason I fell in love with Tom, it's the foundation of my relationships with my sisters, and it's the one thing that cures all. I've learned that if you can laugh during the lowest points in your life, you will always have hope.

I lined the baskets on the dining room table, finished the last load of laundry, and poured myself a glass of sweet tea. I walked out on the front porch and sat down in the rocking chair, then realized that it was almost four-thirty. The girls should be arriving shortly. I was like a little kid anxiously waiting for her friends to arrive. I couldn't contain my excitement.

Tom called to inform me they had arrived safely at Keith's. "Have fun, and *please* be careful," I said, knowing Tom was the biggest kid of all.

"I also wanted to tell you that I got an e-mail from your agent. Apparently, something is wrong with her phone, and she is trying to get a hold of you."

"Tom, do you think she heard from the publisher yet?"

"Baby doll, I don't know, but the easiest way would be to e-mail her and find out."

"Okay, I'm going to right now, and I'll let you know. Have a great time. Call me later," I said as I walked back inside the house and pulled out my laptop.

I sat looking at the computer for a minute before I turned it on. I figured it was another rejection, but honestly, I didn't care. So far, fifteen different publishing companies had rejected my manuscript; yet my agent was always so positive and inspiring. She kept plugging me along and told me to keep an open mind. I wasn't worried so much about getting it published because for me, it was a personal victory. I had achieved my own kind of success. Well, and after fifteen rejections, you come to the conclusion that maybe it wasn't meant for anybody else. I put my heart on paper and relived so many heartbreaking memories. But, the best part about it was that I grew emotionally during the process. My writing helped me deal with the issues I hadn't yet faced. Every time I looked at my manuscript all typed out on my desk, it was like facing a bully and punching his lights out. I was standing up to my self-loathing doubts and the emotional damage I had inflicted upon myself my whole life. With this story, living it and writing it, I had conquered the obstacles that had hindered me before.

Judith had e-mailed me. She informed me of both good news and bad news. I read on with a heavy heart to find my fate. Judith opened the e-mail by emphasizing that I needed to keep an open mind. She said that the publisher wasn't interested but not to give up because J.K. Rowling was rejected many times before someone published her first Harry Potter book. I smiled a close-lipped smile and shook my head, wishing I could be as positive as she was. I appreciated her faith in me.

The good news was that an editor from *Vogue* magazine, who happened to be a good friend of hers, loved my manuscript and adored my attention to detail in clothes. She also loved reading about my sisters. Judith let me know that I was to e-mail her friend because she wanted to talk to me.

Just as I was ready to reply to Judith, I heard a horn beeping in the driveway. I immediately ran to the front door to greet

Fiona with the biggest hug. The e-mail could wait, but my time with my sisters could not.

I may not have my mother, and I will probably never be able to listen to "Silent Night" on Christmas Eve without crying. And I can most likely guarantee that I will probably never be able to look at a Christmas tree and not think of my mom. But through my journey, I have learned that dealing with being sad is a lot easier than dealing with guilt and regret.

My life has been painful at times, and lonely, but it has led me to the person and mother I am proud to be. Helen and Fiona are the greatest gifts my mother gave me, and they continue to help me muddle through my ever-changing emotions, motherhood, and life. And if someone ever asks me how I dealt with my grieving, I will flat out tell them it was the rocks, paper, and flowers that healed me. Most importantly, I know I have salt in my life, and hopefully not pinworms or lice. I'll let you know in three days.

About the Author

Katie Sullivan was raised in the Midwest and grew up in a large close-knit Irish Catholic family. Katie is the mother of three teenagers, and she has been writing since they were babies. Her own mother died when she was young, and Katie realizes the importance of every funny moment and milestone in each of her children's lives. Her personal relationships have had the most impact on her writing. Katie currently resides in Mt. Pleasant, South Carolina and has worked for Charleston County School District for eleven years. She graduated from Wright State University with a degree in History. *Rocks, Paper, Flowers* is her first novel.